Praise for

THERE WILL NEVER BE ANOTHER YOU

"Potent and poignant . . . a remarkable achievement."
—*The Washington Post Book World*

"Carolyn See's unadorned pitch-perfect sentences . . . give the reader as much of a feel for this frightening world as the actual conflicts themselves. See writes about a threatening near-future, but she also writes so well that even her most devastating lines and moments give you hope." —*San Francisco Chronicle*

"The novel's deep resonance lies in [See's] imaginative yet meaningful juxtaposition of global issues and domestic ones: crises in the former can connect with, influence, and even determine the outcome of crises in the latter." —*Booklist* (starred)

"See's ability to intertwine these people's personal worries with a collective sense of dread is what's most impressive here, along with her trademark doomsday pluckiness. She's the best kind of novelist to read in an emergency mood, growing calmer and more self-assured as the anxiety mounts." —Baltimore *Sun*

"Spare and elliptical . . . generous . . . hopeful . . . [*There Will Never Be Another You*'s] quirky twists and turns are closer to life as we know it than the predictable pathways of more conventional fiction." —*The Columbus Dispatch*

"Sardonic but wise, *There Will Never Be Another You* speaks to the inevitability of death and the messy beauty of life."

—Minneapolis *Star Tribune*

"Cool but compassionate . . . [a] psychic snapshot of modern times."

—*More*

"Delightfully satirical."

—*The Boston Globe*

"The bottom-line voice running through this strange and beautiful novel offers exactly as much compromise as Judge Roy Bean would when sending another horse thief off to hang. All to say, *There Will Never Be Another You* is as hard as BBs, and as true. And that, after all, is what you hope for from the first day you sit down to write."

—PETE DEXTER

"I can't think of any novelist remotely like Carolyn See. Who else scares you to death while providing motherly consolation? Who else takes such tremendous risks so tranquilly? Who else writes with such generous courage? There will never be another her!"

—URSULA K. LE GUIN

"Boldly conceived, bravely imagined . . . a darkly visionary, deeply empathic tour de force that embraces both the essential human drama of a domestic tale and the vital issues and broader agendas of a so-called big-picture novel. In her confident marrying of these two often disparate genres, See has crafted an indelible hybrid."

—*Elle*

"See's potent new novel articulates the instinctive, human impulse toward connection in the face of mortality."

—*Publishers Weekly*

ALSO BY CAROLYN SEE

THERE WILL NEVER BE ANOTHER YOU

a novel

CAROLYN SEE

BALLANTINE BOOKS

New York

2007 Ballantine Books Trade Paperback Edition

Copyright © 2006 by Carolyn See

Reading group guide copyright ©2007 by Random House, Inc.

Published in the United States by Ballantine Books, an imprint of The Random House Publishing Group, a division of Random House, Inc., New York.

BALLANTINE and colophon are registered trademarks of Random House, Inc.
READER'S CIRCLE and colophon are trademarks of Random House, Inc.

Originally published in hardcover in the United States by Random House, an imprint of The Random House Publishing Group, a division of Random House, Inc., in 2006.

LIBRARY OF CONGRESS CATALOGING-IN-PUBLICATION DATA

See, Carolyn.
There will never be another you: a novel / Carolyn See.
p. cm.
ISBN 978-0-345-44047-1
1. Widows—Fiction. 2. Volunteer workers in hospitals—Fiction. 3. Parent and adult child—Fiction. 4. California, Southern—Fiction. 5. Crisis management—Fiction. 6. Problem families—Fiction. 7. Dermatologists—Fiction. I. Title.
PS3569.E33T48 2006
813'.54—dc22 2005044932

Printed in the United States of America

www.thereaderscircle.com

2 4 6 8 9 7 5 3 1

Book design by Mary A. Wirth

for

HARVARD and DASH

"You know what?
Even if the business don't work out,
I still got the boat."

—Barfly
Venice, California
2004

2001

AIN'T
NOTHIN'
WE CAN
DO

EDITH

I woke up on the couch, where I'd been sleeping for the last two months. I was alone. I looked at the ceiling for quite a long time and then said, out loud, "Let me just keep my eyes open."

I got up, put on some coffee, pulled on a pair of jeans and a sweatshirt, got out maybe a dozen plastic trash bags, and went into the bedroom where he'd died. I started with the piles of Depends, cartons and cartons of them.

I filled one plastic trash bag with Chux and another with Depends and went out the front door of the apartment to throw the goddamned things down the trash chute. One of my neighbors tottered toward me, snazzy in leopard-skin tights and pearls, even though it wasn't yet six in the morning.

"Well, I made it, Estelle," I said, because Estelle had been telling me for a year now that it was the wives, the caretakers, the relatives, the innocent bystanders, who died first, taking care of their sick husbands. Or whoever. And the husbands went on for-ever. Of course, Estelle's did. He would never die. Just too mean.

"It's not over yet," Estelle said, looking me over, and clicked past, in high heels and rhinestone-spattered socks, using her walker as a weapon.

Inside the apartment, the phone rang. People were savages, re-ally. It was barely six! I took another bag and loaded it up with creams and lotions and antiseptics and catheters of every de-scription, and dozens of those gelled cotton things on sticks that you use to swab the mouths of dying people when water is too much for them. And here was baby powder. And moisturized towelettes.

It took a lot of junk to see someone off to the next world. The den already held two wheelchairs, three sponge-rubber wedges, a trapeze (which had nearly knocked out a nurse when she'd bashed into it one night), two oxygen tanks, a big NO SMOKING sign (even though he'd never used the oxygen and nobody in the house smoked), and an extra commode. I took the other commode and hauled it into the den too, then unhooked the slabs of metal on either side of our bed that had made it into a hospital bed, in the-ory, when you pulled them up, but none of us had ever been able to keep him in anyway. He'd wanted too hard to get out. I'd seen him, when he thought no one was in the room, hoisting himself up against those rails, then failing, sinking back onto the mattress.

But sometimes he succeeded. There he'd be again, down on the floor, and I'd have to call the firemen, who'd pick him up and toss him back in bed.

I hauled the metal sides into the den, and the phone rang again. *Fuck you,* I thought, poured myself some coffee, and sat for ten minutes to read the newspaper. I was putting off the next step, although I knew I had to do it. When the phone rang the third time I went into the bedroom, pulled back the blankets, and stripped the sheets. I knew—I'd read—that when people died they voided everything that was still in them. I had, somewhere in the back of my head, my own suicide plan: pills, vodka, a plastic bag—and for God's sake remember a laxative a day ahead of time—and maybe a Fleet enema. (Although I couldn't imagine, no matter how considerate I might want to be, putting myself through a Fleet when I was going to die anyway.)

But there was nothing here, just a nickel's worth, a modest little stain. I had looked up his behind once, his sphincter helpless, relaxed and open. How much I'll know of you! But it was such a mystery, like a postcard of a subway, pink and clean, curving off into the middle of his body.

As the phone began ringing, I pulled off the sheets, bundled them up with the last set of towels, and walked down to the laundry room. Estelle passed me again, taking her own exercise, keeping herself alive. *See!* her look said, but I ignored her, filled every machine in the place—extra hot water, plenty of bleach.

In the kitchen I threw out the applesauce and the Ensure, the ice cream, in the same way the undertakers had casually taken him out the door the night before. In the bathroom I pitched out the pills to keep his sick heart strong, his blood thin, his pressure down, his flow up. I threw out the laxatives and the powder that slows your bowels to a standstill. I kept the painkillers and the tranquilizers. The hospice people had come yesterday, just minutes after he'd died, to pour what morphine was left in the toilet.

The phone rang. This time I answered. "Yes, what is it," I said resentfully into the receiver, because it wasn't even seven in the morning and I was a widow now and any condolences would have to be pretty good.

"Turn on the television." For a minute, I couldn't even place his voice. The doctor? A neighbor? That infernal minister the hospice people kept sending out, and I couldn't say no because he was part of the package, along with the wheelchairs and the wedges? But no, it was my son. He hadn't even said hello. He sounded more cracked than usual, poor guy. "You'll see history being made, I think." And he hung up.

I poured more coffee, set out some change on the sink to remind me to put the sheets in the dryer when the time came, went into the living room, and turned on the set.

Buildings on fire. In New York. Then one, incredibly, went down.

I admit, for a minute, I was impressed. That was the word. Then I thought, *Fuck that!* The only human being in the world who ever loved me—except for my goofy son, maybe—died last night. Died in my arms. Breathed his last. Excuse me, God, but you're going to have to do better than that if you want to impress me! Damn fucking easterners.

Of course, we all do that now, tell where we were on that date, and what we were doing. I was talking to Melinda Barclay, in the Med Center where I volunteer, to pass the time. We were both still doing it now.

~

THE
LONESOME
ROAD

EDITH

My son persuaded me to take this "volunteer" job to get my mind off things, I guess, but God knows it's the wrong one for me. I sit at this desk and answer questions and kill time writing in this journal. Because I don't knit. A woman "journaling," as if anyone on earth gave a raving shit! Or talking to Melinda. She keeps me company. She's a regular.

I've never liked the sight of blood. And I've never been that crazy about people either. Oh, I like who I like and I try to love who I love, but I think most humans leave something to be desired. Now, in this waiting room, I can see them and hear them spread out along the walls, conversations rising up, peevish and mean. Armenians. Persians. Chinese, a big family—I would bet

Cantonese—a dozen or so: a couple of middle-aged sisters in sleeveless overblouses, crying and soaking up Kleenex; four or five criminal types, young guys covered with tattoos but too shy to venture out into the center of the room. When somebody wants a Coke from the vending machine, one of the sisters goes.

Two different white couples in their forties on the other side of the room, bickering about a restaurant they heard about or went to once. Tre Vignes? Three Vines? Quatro Vignes? No, it was Italian. Quadro? No.

I could tell them. I could walk right over there and say, It's Tra Vignes, up in Napa Valley, a big room, no air-conditioning, art deco bar, great Gorgonzola mousse. My second husband, Charlie, and I went there the summer before he died. But they wouldn't believe me. It's astonishing how often they don't believe me, even when I say, "She's up in Seven thirty-four. Take the elevator to your left and then go right." They think I'm here to give them misinformation, a set of mistakes they can take to a nurse in those silly scrubs they wear now, to get the real scoop, the real deal.

Then again, what do I know? Back when I was one of the people sitting on the couches instead of behind this desk, I watched a huge family go through their dad's seven-hour heart bypass operation. After it was over, they all went out for dinner except for a son-in-law who stayed behind and got busy on his cell phone. "Steven wants to buy razors for everybody in the cast and crew," he said, "but he doesn't want to pay retail." I was so green then, so uninformed about life, that I thought the conversation was about shaving, and thought, Is there really a new kind of luxury item, something wonderfully new to scrape your face and legs? Something good enough for Steven Spielberg to buy? But of course they were scooters, and by the time Charlie was dead those scooters had come—all over the streets everywhere in LA—and just as quickly gone.

The doctors pass through here. My son generally uses a side door, but most of them love to walk through the waiting room. They love the rolling jaunt of it, their white coats streaming out behind them, their laminated badges flapping. They ignore the unfortunates on either side. Or maybe they're teasing, like a stripper. Look while you can, *when* you can, because I'm already *out* of here! They never stop to say hello. It's not in them.

Monsters in white coats walk through here and I know who they are by now. The awful surgeon Shackleford, who shoots African animals on safari and wakes little girls up after their operations to show them color digitized photographs of their own raw flesh; a man who promised a family faithfully he wouldn't take their brother's lung and then went right upstairs and did it, took it right out, because it had an extra-special kind of cancer he was delivering a lecture on later in the summer and the patient couldn't complain, because he was already on a respirator, and then he died.

There are good ones too, of course, the brawny sports orthopedist I caught weeping outside the florist shop at eleven at night, the deeply eccentric internist who wears a beret and can't give anyone bad news. And Dr. Philip Fuchs, my poor movie-star handsome son, who hates sickness—or is it death?—as much as I do, hiding his face when he does happen to walk through here, staring at the floor, shy as a boy at his first prom.

I am a well-groomed woman of sixty-four and a half years. I weigh one hundred and ten pounds. I am a particular kind of Los Angeles lady, the kind with a light tan and blouses of beige silk, very good shoes, a bony face, and a bad disposition. I almost had a "career" once. I was a wife twice. Now I'm a widow. I'm not a crazy white-haired ninny volunteer, the kind they put up on the cardiac ward to raise the general level of insanity. I'm not like the charity fund-raisers who waft through this room on their way to a private lunch (where they serve the same awful salads with fake ranch dressing that suffering families eat in the cafeteria). And I'm not the wretched wife of some celebrity who shows up here to breathe his last, sheltered from the press by his staff and ours alike.

No, I'm just a widow who did paid research for my first husband and entertained very well—effortlessly, it seemed—and charmed my second husband's clients, because it was my job, and raised a son and lived a lucky life until Charlie died.

Then the curtain went up for me (of course you could say it had gone up once before, when my first husband was in his car crash), and I saw the world. Some people would say that's a good thing. That's what they're always saying—that their daughter's brain tumor taught them about God, or their son's lost limbs inspired them to be strong, or their husband's cancer made them into better people. I can't say I feel that way. I know the people in this waiting room don't feel that way. You could say they haven't learned their lessons yet. Maybe I haven't either. I've seen death, the bloodstains of it on our bedroom carpet and on the cobblestones in our apartment driveway and here in this hospital on cold linoleum floors. I learned about the world, what it was made of. I can't say I liked it, or that any of it has done me any good.

All I can do now is divide the world between those who know and those who don't.

Also, the difference between chronic and acute. There's the Barclay family, John and Melinda. Tuesdays, Fridays, Sundays. Dialysis, two years now. Poor Melinda, jittery with badly concealed fear. He leaves her in this big room. She tells him she'll be going out to do some errands or have lunch with a friend, but most of the time she stays, reading or knitting or pacing. Or we talk, if it's slow around here. Twice a week; now it's three. This spring, the end of hot and humid April, her daughter Andrea has been with her, a pretty girl with a good figure and a nice young face. No more than twenty. The doctors have been out a couple of times to talk to the two of them. Swirling, self-important.

But if I hate those doctors so much, those drama kings, why do I stay here? Why do I choose the fate of the volunteer—the witch in the gift shop, the white-haired skeleton up in the cardiac ward? I hate this place! But I can't go back to the position that life is hunky-dory. I have women friends. I give dinner to my son and his wife and kids on some Sunday evenings. But that's not where the truth is.

I'm not saying anyone around here knows the truth either. That flock of chattering Chinese don't know it yet, with some almost brain-dead uncle they've got upstairs. The Barclay family dreads the truth, but the truth is coming to them, walking down the hall to meet them like a bad blind date.

You could say that everyone in this big room has been phoned up by the truth. They've come here with rage or fear or resignation—or curiosity, maybe: *Is this what it is?*

As I say, I had a clue about it once. Actually, twice—no, three times. After Hamilton's crash. Again for about ten minutes after my first granddaughter was born and lay on my daughter-in-law's chest, and we, all of us there, spoke in tongues and knew the truth. And the third time, for about ten days, as my darling second husband died.

I know these worries about mortality, life and death, are nothing new. If I want to get to know death on a really friendly basis, why not go to Mexico and help out in a clinic? I'm interested in the distractions up here, I guess, the puffs of red smoke the doctors and their entourages send up. I watch medical shows on television now with amusement and interest. Where's the boredom? I ask the actors on *E.R.* Or, when that man on public television droned on about hospice a few years ago, Where's the blood? Where's the shit? Where's the terror? Where's the *death*?

You could say I'm stuck. "You're stuck," I often say to my reflection in my dressing room at home, as I button my blouse, pull up my good slacks with killer creases, put on my sweater, slip into my good brown pumps with the low Cuban heels.

I assume my family thinks I'm doing well, imposing order on my life. Staying out of the way and out of their hair. If they think of me at all.

And I do go out. I pride myself on it. With men as gallant and forlorn as old cars.

But I'm stuck! I can't go inside, upstairs, and I can't go home.

I'm not going up to the cardiac wing or the cancer wing because I've seen enough, more than enough. I can't go up to obstetrics because I suspect there's a lie in there, many lies. It's not necessarily good news to be born. And I'm not going home to what was. It will be awhile, if ever, before I look at a new recipe or buy new linens or even plant new flowers, because every flower holds a death inside it. Every newborn is a person waiting to die. Like *this* is news!

EDITH

Two months after Charlie died, I asked an old high school friend over to watch the Grammys—the Tonys? something—on television. I know widows who waited less than a week to hop in the sack with someone, and more power to them! There has to be an antidote to this death thing. Besides, in those days, the whole country was tuning up to die—remember that anthrax scare? We were even afraid to open a letter. So I called up my old friend and asked him over.

The minute he came in the door, I knew it was a terrible mistake. The screen door opened and he brought in a burst of fresh air with him. He was wearing a tweed jacket; he carried a bag of deli stuff in one arm and a couple of bottles of wine in the other.

Still, he managed to give me a brotherly hug. I thought the odds were two to one I'd begin to cry and not be able to stop.

My dad would come in the door after a day of work, wearing tweed, smelling of scotch and tobacco backed by that raw refreshing burst of chilly night air, and he'd hug me. Even my first husband, for all his affectations and quirks (and mine too), would slip through the door, usually in a good mood and wearing tweed and carrying food, and he'd give me an easy kiss and then grab up our little boy and swing him around, make a big deal of it, always with that backdraft of fresh air, breaking the boredom of a day at home.

And then Charlie for all those years and years, coming home in his brown suede jacket, never without food or drink or some kind of present: a toaster with room for four slices, or a yo-yo or Slinky or Hot Wheels for Phil, who wasn't even his child. . . .

Here it was again, the crack of a screen door against wood, the rush of cold air, and I was so threatened by tears and that smell of tweed that I could only say, "You go on into the living room; I'll take care of all this," and took the sacks from him.

So, of course he did, and sat down in Charlie's chair, and turned on the television to watch the underdressed girls on the red carpet while I opened the coleslaw and salad and laid out the sandwiches and poured the wine, and thought, *I'm right back at the beginning. This is where I came in; this is the start of the movie one more time, but I'm so sick of this movie!*

But I didn't want a repetition of my mother's last years, a widow among widows, going to sleep at seven o'clock at night because there was no reason to stay up and nothing to stay up for, and then waking at two or three in the morning to read until dawn. I wouldn't let my home get *strange,* with peanut butter on the bathroom sink, or ice packs in the freezer where food ought to be, or stacks of newspapers and old mail on the dining room table, because there was no one there to tell me not to do it or because the dining room table wasn't there for eating anymore, or with the sheets on the other side of the bed remaining clean, perfectly clean, unslept-in clean.

I knew what I was *not* going to do, would not under any circumstances do; I didn't have the faintest clue about what I was supposed to do. But it sure wasn't going to be carrying in sandwiches to an old guy—even though he was only my friend from long ago—while he sat planted by the television like a bad cartoon of an oblivious husband.

I sat down at the other end of the couch, thinking, It's not even this guy's fault. All I have to do for the rest of this evening is keep from crying like a fool and be civil until all the awards get given out, do the right thing, because he only thinks he's being kind to an old friend, and he brought the sandwiches.

In the big apartment—filled, I saw again, with all Charlie's possessions, his taste, his kind soul, even though I'd gone for years absently thinking everything was *my* stuff—my friend seemed awed, sad, tentative. The walls of books and posters that had seemed—what a joke!—warm and cozy when Charlie was alive turned the place into a vast, gloomy church, almost Gothic. When he spoke, my old friend's voice came out as a reverent whisper.

Is there really anything like a broken heart? I thought I'd been doing pretty well, but there was something definitely bad going on in my chest, not a break, more like a big chunk of ice. And it was strange because that cold came out as heat in my face, which was scalding, stinging behind my eyes. I didn't have to talk, thank God; there was the television. The program would be over by ten o'clock. I could get my old friend out the door by eleven.

From far away at the other end of the couch came the sound of my old friend's life story, beautifully told. An affair with someone he'd loved greatly, a courtyard in central Europe, the sluice of a gentle fountain, the reasons why he and she couldn't marry. They were endless. His regrets. His longing.

Then he said, sadly, "I could have been the leader of the Romanian Jews."

That's it, I thought. I really am going out of my mind. But after a few minutes it became more clear. He meant he could have been the leader of the Romanian Jewish *prop masters*. He had lost a union election; it hadn't even been close. In fact, he thought, the fix was in. There had to have been a conspiracy. He was sure of it.

"I know there will be some people who say I shouldn't vote Green," he said, "the world being what it is today. But I have to go with my conscience."

"Just don't *tell* anybody," I snapped. "There's no reason why you have to tell anybody!"

But of course the whole point of voting Green was so you *could* tell somebody.

At eleven, I gave him the boot.

"Can't I even watch the news? I don't have a television at home." That was the real reason he had come over. A man his age, without a TV!

"You have to go home," I said. "I'm tired now. It was really fun. Thanks so much. I mean it. It was fun to have you over."

His old, sweet, familiar face filled with concern. He was handsome, more than when he was young, the kind of man who'd grown into his looks.

"Look," he said. "I want to tell you how sorry I am. A lot of my friends are widows now. I know you've had a hard go of it. I'm willing to be your friend. I'm *glad* to be your friend, and help you out any way I can. You know, if there's anything you need. . . ."

Back inside I stood by Charlie's bed, bent over his pillow. He wasn't there, in any way, shape, or form. I let the grief come out, about an hour of howling and gasping, nothing really personal.

So I waited awhile before I tried it again, I told Melinda. But then I did it again. I couldn't stand to be alone.

He stood outside the condominium doors, posing, his craggy face turned to the right. He wore a black turtleneck, black leather jacket, black leather pants and boots. He looked great. His white hair, combed back over his collar, carried a natural curl. His mouth, which had been described in print as cruel and selfish by so many heartbroken women, seemed OK to me.

I pushed through the condominium doors. He might have been pretending not to see me. I didn't look so bad myself.

He took hold of my hand—my right hand—with his left, or at least he tried. Our fingers wouldn't go together. His arm was too long, or short; my arm was too short, or long. We walked to where he had parked his black Range Rover, no more than twenty,

twenty-five feet away, but it felt like eternity. Finally, he let go of my hand to help me inside. He had to. My skirt wasn't full and needed to be hiked up.

"I thought we'd go to a little place in the Palisades people have told me about," he said. "Modo Mio."

"That's nice," I said. "That's a nice place. That's fun. Very good food. Northern Italian."

He looked straight ahead and drove. "I'm a little deaf," he said, "in my left ear. Have been for a long time now."

I thought about it. I remembered a hell dinner party we'd gone to in the year before Charlie had died. I'd had Charlie—deaf but cunning about it—on my left at the head of the table, conducting a masculine monologue designed not to leave room for questions. Across from me, our beautiful hostess sat, smiling and determined. To her left, her own husband, deaf, almost blind, and very sloppy, with a good portion of the night's dinner already spread across his pale blue cashmere sweater. Farther on down the table, another determined wife and her bedraggled spouse. "Al's been a little quiet since his stroke," our hostess whispered. What she meant was that Al hadn't spoken a word in years.

To my own right that night sat a city-renowned psychiatrist, therapist to the stars, *really* stone deaf. Used to Charlie, I leaned into him, enunciating slowly, placing my mouth close to his ear. "There's no need to do that," the psychiatrist said. "I can read lips perfectly well." So I'd sat back and talked to him, but he hadn't read one word. "I can't understand you," he had said. "Speak up!"

"I have this SUV so I can transport my paintings," my date said.

"That's *good,*" I said. "It's very nice."

He coughed. "I've been having trouble with my lungs," he said. "I have a lung infection. I've had them all my life."

"That's *bad,*" I said. "Are you taking antibiotics?"

"Of course," he answered, and we were more or less quiet until we reached Modo Mio. It was so interesting. When you came in with a stranger, waiters pretended not to know you.

"I don't need a menu," the painter said. "Just tell me the specials."

How hard it was. How hard it was going to be.

The waiter, avoiding my eye, recited them.

"I don't read, you know," the painter said, after we'd ordered. "Never have. They used to call me Dopey when I was growing up. My family. And my teachers. Because I couldn't read."

I'd sat to his right in the car and to his right, now, in the restaurant. Wasn't the right his good ear? Did he have one?

He told me his life story, efficiently edited so that it ended about the time our appetizers came. He'd been disrespected in high school and by his family, joined the service, actually learned to read a little bit, then came home and taken advantage of the GI Bill. He'd accidentally enrolled in an art class, thinking it was an art *history* class and all he'd have to do was look at slides. Then there he was, on that first day, at an absolute loss, with sheets of paper on an easel in front of him and jars of paint. The professor began to move around the classroom, making scathing remarks, and in a panic the young student had reached into the jars with his fists, smearing and streaking the white paper like a madman.

The professor had stopped, pulled the work from the easel,

and pinned it to a corkboard. *"This!"* he'd said. "This is how you do it!"

The marinated mushrooms came, and the bruschetta.

"I'm sorry, I just have to ask this," I said. "They say you're a heartbreaker. That you go to the restroom in restaurants and then climb out the window. That you abandon the women you date."

"What?"

"Is it true that you shimmy out the window? *Climb out the window at restaurants?*"

He coughed. "I get bored easily," he said. "That's true."

He spent the time between the appetizers and the entrees talking about how his one true wish, now he was older, was to live on Capri.

"I'd have eight women," he said. "I think that's just about right. You could be the head of all of them. Keep them in line. You seem pretty organized."

"Do the laundry and cooking?" I asked.

"Make *them* do it! You're a nice woman. Put together. I like that, especially at our age."

He was killingly handsome in the candlelight. And he was quite famous. He didn't ask me about myself, but I put it down to his deafness. The deaf are perfectly fine as long as they keep talking, I knew. It's only when they have to listen that they get in trouble.

I concentrated on this guy's good ear, pitching sound waves at him. My life story, short and sweet, including my son and my husbands. I finished up by the time we'd ordered coffee. We didn't want dessert.

I thought about going home, how hard it was to be alone and keep on being alone.

"I'd like to see your paintings sometime," I said.

But he'd had enough, for that night at least.

I didn't see the painter again for about six months. Then, with a lady friend, I attended the opening of an "installation" in Beverly Hills. It wasn't art in the usual sense of pictures on walls, or even sculptures on pedestals, but an enormous assemblage of airplane parts, old, privately owned planes in shades of faded turquoise and dusty pink, beginning at the center of the room and branching out, with the aid of hundreds of metal pulleys and cables, into the far corners of the roof of the room. Looking like the end of the world.

My friend and I saw him and went over to say hello. He'd had a bad bout with prostate cancer and looked frail and drawn. But he still wore his leathers and held his chin at a brave angle.

"You know, girls," he said, "I can see you now as human beings instead of just women. I never could do that before. It's strange."

"Well, thank you, dear," my friend said, "that's a real compliment!" And kissed him on the cheek. So did I.

I laid off dating for a while, thinking, A woman doesn't need a man to get along in this world!

My son took to inviting me over in the middle of the week for dinner. But frankly, Melinda, it was a nightmare. His wife—well, his wife! She's a nut job, and the world situation hasn't helped her disposition any. I love my grandson, Vernon, he was always a darling kid, but he's going through a phase now. And Eloise is thirteen; that's all you need to know about that. . . .

She nodded her head, but she wasn't listening. Wondering, I guess, if she'd be reduced to going to a restaurant someday with a man who didn't love her, who might excuse himself and then shimmy out a restroom window. Wondering if—or when—it would come to that.

PHIL

He saw the first cat on his way to work about seven in the morning. It was gray against the gray of the curb, barely visible paws,
limbs stretched to the maximum that only happens when cats die,
its furry face not visible. Then he drove past and it was gone.

He saw his morning's patients, dropped down to the cafeteria
for coffee and a sandwich, sat alone by the window, looked out,
and saw another one, black, lined up against a shrub, creating its
own shadow; you could hardly see the thing. But it didn't look
good. He went back upstairs, holding his food in the elevator;
he'd finish eating back at his desk.

From his office window he saw another, lopped over in the
crotch of a tree—or no, it was farther up, really, out on a branch

near the top. And he could see its face this time, pulled back in a grimace, jaws set wide. God!

It made him go out and ask Kathi if she'd noticed anything.

"Did you see those cats?"

She stopped what she was doing on the computer and looked at him.

"I'm sorry?"

"Those cats. I saw three dead cats this morning."

"I hate those things. The way people come out here and feed them. They're wild. And dirty."

"Well, three of them are dead now. I saw three."

"Probably some kind of distemper."

"Do you think we ought to call somebody? Somebody to pick them up?" By *we,* he meant her, of course.

She gave him a thoughtful look and picked up the phone.

"This is Dr. Fuchs's office down in the Medical Center? Doctor says he's seen three dead cats just this morning and someone ought to pick them up." She looked up at him again. *Where?* she mouthed.

He told her. She repeated it to the person on the other end of the line. "Yes. Because he says it's a health hazard, at the very least."

He went back into his office and sipped at his cooling coffee. Not much to do. He went out past his receptionist again and picked up a magazine—*Outdoor*—and took it back inside with him. And looked absently, again, out his window.

A cherry picker had gotten here in record time and was creaking cautiously up into the tree outside and below his window. The guy in the picker was dressed in white, in what looked like a HAZ-MAT outfit except it didn't have any lettering, and his face was covered with a clear plastic mask. He was using pincers about three feet long. He reached gingerly out to the branch, pinched the cat, brought it back in to the platform he was standing on, and—Phil saw now—dropped it onto a stack of what had to be maybe eighteen or twenty other cats.

Phil picked up the phone and called his pal Fred, in the next wing. "Hey. Have you seen the cats?"

A female voice answered. "He stepped out of the office. May I have him call you back?"

"Uh, Nikki, this is Dr. Fuchs. If you'd have him give me a call back at his convenience. . . ."

But when Fred called back it was his own turn to be with a patient, and they played tag like that until close to five that afternoon. One of his patients did mention that he'd seen two Animal Control trucks pulled up to the Emergency Room entrance, and could it be something like a pit bull attack? Because why else would they be there?

Phil got scared. He called Felicia.

"What is it?" she said. "What's wrong?"

"Have you seen anything weird on television?"

"No, I've been out. I got all the knives sharpened. It cost seventy-two dollars! But you know that nick in the ham knife? They smoothed it over. It looks brand-new."

"That's good," he said.

"What's *wrong*?" Her voice was sharp.

"Nothing. I may be a little late, is all. Not too late. Maybe an hour."

"You be sure and call me. Is it a brush fire? Do you want me to see if there's a brush fire?"

"It's nothing, honey."

He went into a cubicle where a truly awful case of psoriasis universalis was waiting for him. Like a Hiroshima victim. His stomach tightened some more. This was just a kid, maybe in his twenties. Phil had tried a lot of treatments: saltwater baths, UV rays, whatever. The kid just got worse.

"You know, Jason, there's another thing we can try. It's kind of drastic, but it could be worth it. There are some hot springs in Mexicali; you go there for twenty-one days. You soak all day, and the condition gets better. You think your mother might be up for going with you? Sometimes just getting out of where you are can be a big help. There's some mixture of minerals—they can't duplicate it, but they know it works and they say it lasts. I can get you copies of some of the research."

Big heavy tears rolled down the kid's cheeks and dropped onto his raw chest. "It's not going to work," he cried. "Nothing's going to fix this."

"Ah, *come* on, Jason. Don't say that."

He knew he should touch the kid, take hold of his shoulder, pat him on the back, something. But he couldn't.

He wrote out a prescription for a stronger ointment. Waited for the kid to put on his shirt. Even looked, not so covertly, at his watch. Picked up the cubicle phone when it rang.

"Can you get out for a drink?" Fred's voice. Research scientist. Spent his days with rabbits and chickens.

"I'm with the last patient of the day."

"Good. Outside the main doors in fifteen minutes."

"There's something I want to ask you about." He watched the kid tuck in his shirt, duck his head to look in the wall mirror, run a comb through his hair.

"On the steps. Fifteen minutes."

Fred was waiting for him. Five o'clock. Time for a drink. They started walking south, toward downtown Westwood, down long shallow cement steps, across the big brick hospital courtyard.

"Did you hear?" Fred asked.

"I was going to ask you." His heart, his stomach clenched.

"They screwed up."

"Who?"

"Someone in the bio lab. They're having a shit fit over there. We're all locked out."

"Is that what it is with the cats?"

"Yeah. As long as it just stays with the *cats*. It started with some monkeys, or so I've been hearing, this long afternoon."

"A virus? Bacteria?" Phil tried to keep his voice steady.

"They're not saying."

"Who's the *they*?"

"Guys I know. And a secretary. And I talked to one of the Animal Control people."

"The Palomino?" Their favorite place to drink, down in the Village.

"Sure."

It was five blocks away, downhill. Walking back to their cars would give them a chance to sober up a little.

"What about the media? Shouldn't someone tell them what's going on?"

"We don't *know* what's going on."

They walked in silence, past pedicure parlors and movie theaters and fast-food restaurants—Westwood was nothing like the pretty little California college town he remembered from his youth—and went in gratefully through Palomino's big doors into a big room and up to a long, swank, curving bar. Big abstract paintings covered the walls. Manet reproductions, Leger. They both ordered martinis.

"It could just be distemper."

"Or someone got sick and tired of all the feral cats on campus."

"Sure."

"Well, a lot of people don't like them. Kathi doesn't like them."

Fred looked interested. "Want to go find out about the monkeys?"

"*Hell,* no!"

"You said you'd only be an hour."

"Is there anything on television?"

"What is it! What's wrong? There's *nothing* on television.

Nothing worse than usual. I gave the kids their dinner. I don't know how it's stood up. Mussels in white wine and cream. I'm afraid it might have curdled, just a little."

Phil, sitting up at the kitchen bar—since it was just the two of them—looked down, distressed, at the mussels, their pouty mouths, the juice.

"Did you know, in the influenza epidemic back in 1918, that guys fainted when they did the autopsies? Because the lungs they looked at had all turned blue."

"Phil! *What is it?* Why can't you tell me what's *going on*?"

"It's nothing. It isn't anything. I'm sure." Then he told her about the cats.

"Why didn't you call Administration? Tomorrow you can call Animal Control, find out what happened. Probably somebody just got sick of those cats. They *are* all over the place, over there. You know, you get worked up over things that aren't really bad. You know you do." She tried their old joke. "You know you should have gone into law!"

Their stove, one of those restaurant stoves, gleamed. She shivered and put her hand over her mouth, reached out with the other to grab him. She felt electric, foreign. He kept his own hand completely motionless, until she drew back.

"Shall we leave now?" she asked him. "Shall we just put the kids in the car and *drive*?"

His stomach did another clench and he went to the freezer to pull out the gin. "Don't be ridiculous," he said.

"Well, *that* doesn't help anything. If you're going to drink, at least it should be red wine. For your heart."

She was so stupid sometimes. "I know that!"

"You don't *act* like you know it."

He turned on the kitchen television, the baby one on the sink. But they wouldn't have anything on CNN. Because if anything really was happening, someone would be keeping it a secret. He switched to look for local news but it was the wrong time for it, and the network news wouldn't be on until eleven. If there was going to be news anywhere, it would be local. Escaped monkeys, maybe. Dead cats, maybe. A suspicious poisoner. "Do we have a radio around here?"

"Upstairs. You *know* that. In our bedroom. On the closet shelf by your workout clothes." She took away his mussels, sent them clattering back into the pot.

But he didn't feel like going upstairs. Something about not wanting to be alone in the dark. Afraid he'd get sick, catch whatever they'd let loose. Afraid he was going to die. He looked over at Felicia, trying to think of a way to tell her, to let her in on his terrible not-*that*-unreasonable fear, but as he looked at her he could see only light glancing and reflecting off her face, which was made of skin and flesh. If anything, she was more spooked than he was. She was talking to him, but her mouth looked like an awful sore. He couldn't look at her. He had to turn his head away. He *was* zoning out, was zoned out, but there wasn't much he could do about it. Nothing he wanted to do about it. When they'd first had Vern tested for ADHD, the docs had asked some insulting questions: a genetic component, maybe?

So he fell back on his genetic component. Turned to stone. That was all he could do.

"Could you get the radio for me?" he said, out into the middle space of the kitchen. "I'm bushed. I'd really appreciate it." In the time she was gone, he could fill up his glass with gin, drink it down, fill it again.

He knew she was tired of his shenanigans. She'd almost had it—not necessarily with him but with his scenes, his irrationality, his fears, his nerves. Whatever it was that made him a mama's boy, whatever it was that made it so he couldn't measure up to his father. Whichever father. He got on her nerves these days, whatever he did. They were bad for each other.

"It could be nothing," he said. "We've just watched too much television. I can't believe—"

"Believe what? Believe what! You just told me there *wasn't* anything to worry about. Didn't you? Just some stray cats. But Phil? Are *you* sick? I mean, *really*? Is there something really wrong with you and you aren't *telling* me?"

He looked away from her, somewhere in the space between him and the stove. "Get me the radio. Can't you do that for me?"

She left the room. He zoomed over to the fridge, opened it, poured. Drank. Poured.

The phone rang. He picked it up, knowing it would be Fred.

"So I went back tonight. Took a walk through some of the labs. Told them I had to check up on my rabbits. Wore my white coat. My God, Phil!"

"Did you find out anything?"

"Yeah."

"What?"

"Some stuff. What *wasn't* there. But I don't really know."

"What?" The gin blurred his vision. His blood pressure was rising, he knew it. Maybe he'd have a heart attack.

"I found the monkey place."

Phil waited.

"Do you ever wonder if it's safe now to talk on phones? I know it's paranoid, but sometimes I wonder. If it's safe to talk on phones."

Something about this made Phil realize he wasn't the only one a little bit drunk. Something about how Fred said *ph-ones.*

"There was a great big room, full of empty cages. And a desk for the graduate student, or whoever; there wasn't anybody at the desk. All the lights were way bright. I could see that through the window. The door was locked but I used my master key and got in. There were only two or three monkeys left in there and I *know* I heard it was some kind of a big experiment. A big deal they had going on. There was a lot of vomit and shit around. Nobody'd cleaned it up. . . ."

"Maybe—they just . . . died?"

"Maybe. But there wasn't anybody there or anybody working on records or anybody cleaning up. Or anybody. And there are some windows in there, Phil. Windows to the outside."

"Open or closed?"

"Closed. But—you know."

"Well."

"Yeah, I know. I'll be saying good night now."

The way he said it, *good night now,* like somebody's aunt or uncle, stayed with Phil, stuck in his throat as he poured another drink, checked to see that the kids were OK, then went in to be with Felicia, who looked more like his wife now, more like the woman he married, tumbled back into their bed, sound asleep, her mouth open, the portable radio held tight to her ear.

He undressed, got into bed, took the radio, took a turn listening. She had it on KNX, all news all the time, but it was only about car chases and gang killings. Feeling a little better, after a while, he went to sleep.

The next day he called over to Fred's office and was told by Nikki, "The doctor's at home. He's got a touch of the flu, he says."

And the day after that, "He's had a family emergency. He's been called home to Port Townsend. His father called to tell me."

And then, a few days later when he called, a mechanical UCLA voice said that the extension was no longer in use.

That was the end of Fred. Phil hadn't known him that well anyway.

And the UCLA feral cats. Because they died right off.

Animal Control trucks roamed Westwood for a while. But after a while they went away.

EDITH

It could be said that my son is the curse of my life. If there is an accident to be had, he will have it. When he was eight, we were in one of those paintball salons—they were new then—and he sailed right into a wall and knocked himself out. He needed twenty-six stitches. Two years later, away at summer day camp, he went horseback riding, wearing shorts, and while the other little boys stuck to the road—trail, whatever—he wandered off, found a barbwire fence, rode up against it, and tore his right thigh to shreds. A camp counselor fainted when Phil got back to the group—fell right off his horse and got his own concussion.

What else? I can't even begin. Just recently, I mean in the past year, he was returning a grocery cart in a parking lot and went straight into one of those metal cart holders, banged himself in the forehead, and came home with a lump the size of a goose egg. His wife phoned to tell me, as if it were my fault, when *she's* the one who—oh, here I go!—won't lift a finger in the house. The day she married Phil they got through the ceremony all right (she did look absolutely beautiful that day), but after the deal was done, she turned, looked around the church, went the color of yogurt, and fainted dead away. One of her beaded slippers fell off. I guess you could call it the Gypsy's warning.

On the other hand.

On the other hand, when he was fourteen he brought that friend of his home from school, someone who'd been beaten up pretty harshly by his dad, and insisted—*just insisted*—that we keep him at the house for a week. We couldn't call a doctor or even a social worker. He took care of the kid himself, bandaging his cuts and so on, and got the kid to call his grandparents to work something out, some new living arrangements. And it did work out. And Phil did it when he was just a kid himself.

And he does know a lot about wine. That counts for something in the world we live in. He's not pretentious about it. He just—likes it.

He was king of his junior prom back in high school. I can remember how he looked that night, or maybe it's only the pictures I remember. He had the most open face! Just a lot of red-brown curls spilling over his forehead and over his ears and a big wide grin and his arm around—whatever her name was; prom queen is all I can remember. He glowed when he was a kid. He had pink cheeks. Now he goes from pale to florid in a minute's time. Florid from tennis, pale from staying hours under those lights.

He saves his money but he's not stingy.

He's sad, that's what makes him pale. I hardly ever see him laugh. Maybe he does when he's at home or when he's at work, but I can't imagine it. I don't see the lines there, the lines in his face from laughing.

I don't see meanness or impatience either. Only worry, sometimes, and sadness.

It makes me so mad sometimes. Because this is our one and only life, Melinda! He knows that as well as I do. He's been there when people die. He *must* know—he's selling himself short—that he could be so much more than he is.

He took a wrong turn.

Maybe it's that wife of his. I've never been able to stand that woman!

But it's none of my business. He wanted to marry her and he did, and that's it; it's over.

I *know* he shouldn't have had kids. He worries too much, and he's not tough enough on them.

And God knows, he's had to put up with me; I'm not the easiest person to live with. But, my God, at least I *fight* life a little bit. I don't just lie down and take it.

You know what it is? He's too handsome. He's got smooth skin and those dark blue eyes, and he's still got all his hair but with just a little silver over the ears, and he's got that *forlorn* look, that lost look. It's a wonder the women aren't all over him—well, maybe they are. What do I know?

What do we ever really know about the people close to us?

It's hard having sons, if you're a mother. Stay away from them and you're cold, withholding, whatever. Do you know what John Kennedy said about his mother? "She was never there for me, never!" As if she didn't have a dozen other kids and that husband of hers. As if he wasn't already the President of the United States!

But if you stay close to them, if you love them and make the mistake of showing it, then you're tying them up with apron strings; what a concept! You're making them into mama's boys. You're stunting their growth, you're—I don't know. You're ruining their lives, one way or another.

Phil loved his real dad, that learned man whose nose was always in a book and who criticized my flower arrangements but who did dote, unstintingly, on his son and told him stories of King Arthur and spoke to him of nobility and how he should strive to have "ferocious good manners." Well, that was over soon enough. Death by car crash. Over and out.

Phil made up his mind to love his stepfather too. God knows *I* loved him. I picked Charlie because he wasn't charming on purpose. Because he said what he meant and meant what he said. He was kind to Phil.

Later, they always shook hands when they saw each other. Phil, big and so beautiful and kind of gappy, as though there were holes in him (even though he put on some weight after he married Felicia), and Charlie, chunky and dense, making a small fortune in construction, always willing and able to talk about sports, although a little shaky about the Lakers. Never thinking of a word to say to Felicia or the children, but then why should he?

When Charlie first got sick, Phil rose to the occasion, or tried to. Phil was a doctor at UCLA; he knew what it was to die in a hospital. Thank God it wasn't cancer, just a bum ticker, a bad heart. So Charlie stayed home, definitely not the life of the party, just as often wearing his pajamas, watching the Sports Channel or Comedy Central.

When things got worse, Phil came over every night and every morning to help take care of him. He had no aptitude at all for what he was doing. He'd frog-march Charlie out of bed and into the shower, sit him in a plastic chair, and turn the water on full blast—without getting it warm first. He'd scrub Charlie's back with a loofah, forgetting—and Phil's a dermatologist!—that old skin is thin skin. He'd haul him out and over onto the toilet, waiting for Charlie to move his bowels, which sometimes happened, sometimes didn't. He'd pull out Charlie's electric shaver, forgetting that shavers don't work that well on wet skin. He'd say, "Don't worry, Mom, we guys can get this done on our own." Heroically, he'd wipe Charlie's ass, pull on Depends, wrap him in clean pajamas, and haul him back, like some old drunk, into the bed, which I would have made up in the meantime.

Charlie liked to be up and about. He'd crawl halfway out of bed and get stuck there. One time, early on, when I wanted to call the fire department, he gave me a piece of his mind. "Absolutely not! Get Phil," he'd say. "Phil can handle it." So, for those first several months, I'd call my son at the office and get his receptionist. She's a nice woman, always patient with me, but she thought I took advantage of him. I'd wait for Phil to make the drive over, buzz himself in, say, "Where's Charlie?" and scope out the details.

If his left leg is here and his right leg is *there,* how can we make it work so that, together, we can heave him back into bed?

Once Charlie inched his way down, down, down toward the foot of the bed. I was at home with him, but sometimes I'd be on the phone or talking to the part-time housekeeper.

Or there were days when I raced out, hoping Charlie would just stay in bed and not wander off. One day I came home, and as I unlocked the front door there he was, dressed in a sport shirt and his old brown suede jacket and nothing at all on the bottom, and I said, rather crabbily, "Where do you think you're going?" And he answered, "To the game, of course. The big game." And as I was half leading, half hauling him back into the bedroom, he said, "Just answer me this. Are we in Green Bay or not?"

But on this one day he'd gotten down to the bottom of his bed, and I hadn't even gone anywhere. I'd been puttering, opening the mail maybe, in that half-conscious trance the living get into when they're with someone who's dying. I knew what he was up to, in a limited sort of way. I'd go in every fifteen minutes or so and say, "Wouldn't you rather be up a little farther on your pillows?" He'd allow himself to be propped up, just a little, but then he'd begin to slide back down. And then I went in to check on him and he'd slid halfway off the bed. He'd counted on being able to lift himself to a standing position when he got that far, but it wasn't going to happen; he didn't have the strength. He'd taken off his pajama top and his white skin was gleaming, his pacemaker in plain sight like a great big wristwatch.

"Can't move," he said.

"Could you just scoot back up? Something like that?" I'm not the angel type, I'm sorry to say. Certainly not then.

"Nothing to scoot," he said.

"I'm calling the fire department," I said. "This is ridiculous. And I'm hiring a nurse. I mean it. I can't be doing this."

"No!" he said. "Call Phil. He'll take care of me."

"He works! He's got a job! I can't"—I almost said *bother* but I couldn't do it—"I can't be calling him all the time at work."

"Call Phil."

It was maybe five in the afternoon. I thought with rage about Felicia. Did she ever *once* call up and ask if I needed anything? But I knew that was bogus even as I thought it. I had my own friends to help me, I wasn't as bad off as I might be. And yes, I could have called in nurses or helpers or caretakers or even hospice, but Charlie didn't want it. Wasn't ready for it.

So I wasn't going to do it.

It was six at night by the time Phil got there. When he came in he said, "For God's sake, Ma!"

"I know, I *know*," I answered him. "But he wouldn't let me call anybody but you."

"I *can't* be—"

"I *know*," I said. "Leave it alone."

"Where do I start?"

We looked at him and at each other and we both started to laugh. Even Charlie tried out a sorrowful smile.

"OK. You take his left arm and I'll take the right. One, two, three, *pull*!"

Nothing.

"Oh," Charlie said. "Oh."

I left the room. I couldn't be a part of it. A few minutes later, when I came back, somehow they were *standing* together, staggering around on top of the bed.

"Make him lie down!" I said, and they both buckled over. Phil sprained his wrist on the end table.

We got the covers pulled up over Charlie, who began to snore like a truck.

"Can I get you an Ace bandage for that?" His arm was already beginning to swell. Little specks of blood were beginning to appear, beneath the skin.

"No. I've got to get home."

"Well, go *on* then!"

Phil's sensitive, too sensitive. And when I look—or try to look—at him, just the person, straight on, he's doing all right, more than all right.

So why does he drive me nuts? Why do I sound so critical of him?

Because I see his sadness, like a cut. Like a cut I can't fix. I can't bandage him, or take him in, like he did with that kid so long ago. I see him walking through his life with that sad absent-minded look. There's no prom king about him now. He's what you'd call an average Joe. He's settled for that and maybe something worse. He's like a beaten dog, sometimes, or a horse in Central Park.

Was it something I did?

Without meaning to do it?

Or is it that wife of his?

Just thinking about it drives me crazy! That's why, sometimes, even though I know it's ungrateful and unmotherly and God knows what else, I think of my son as a curse. My own personal curse. And the only person on earth anymore that I love, except for Vern, maybe.

PHIL

Maybe it was their last name: Fuchs, a family blight. Loyalty to his dead father had kept him through the years from changing it. Some teacher's aide back when he was in kindergarten had called it what it probably really was, Philip Fucks, and that had been the ending—or the start—of his grade school career, maybe his life's career. It had condemned him to life as a buffoon, the last bewildered one to get a joke.

"Don't take that crap!" his stepdad had said to him, or even, "Beat the crap out of them!" But Phil couldn't think of it. Back in medical school he'd taken the least scary way out, first deciding to be an obstetrician but nixing that after a week of looking up women's things all day, watching them swell up and turn purple and out jumped a baby. It was too nerve-racking. He settled finally on dermatology, since nobody ever died of a rash, and he could refer the melanomas to oncology.

His stepdad—trying to be kind—had said marrying Felicia would put some backbone in him, and now Phil thought that was a good idea in theory, looking at her across a gleaming tablecloth that had belonged to her mother. What really happened was that she didn't have much backbone either. She took care of things like health and clothes and running the house. She'd thrown a lot of tantrums lately.

Dinner tonight was steamed boneless chicken breasts, steamed beets, steamed broccoli: one of Felicia's random health experiments. They all tried to live well. He played tennis twice a week and ran on weekends, and the kids played soccer. At least Eloise did, who lounged in her chair now, ignoring this awful dinner, playing with her upper lip. Philip couldn't even say, *Can't you cut that out*? because he was afraid of his daughter's sneer. Eloise sneered because she was a good athlete and a first-rate scholar. She'd made it into Brentwood School, ninth grade now, and was a goddess in her mother's eyes.

Phil eyed his chicken and took a deep drink of his Chateau St. Jean, which he'd read about—and since then dreamed of—as the perfect accompaniment to stuffed foie gras. His wine collection was his luxury and consolation, and Felicia put up with it because it was an OK thing to do in their circle of friends. A lack of candles made them all look out of sorts tonight. Felicia picked at her chicken, her mouth turned down at both corners. She was one of those women who'd have to get a face-lift quick and early, and he knew exactly what she'd look like then: not good-humored, because she had a sad, stubborn streak in her, but determined, with everything on her face going *up*.

How he'd like some candles or some music! But this was an early weeknight dinner. All business. Just beyond his wineglass and his water glass and salad, he was treated to the sight of his son Vernon's hair, black and pressed down against the tablecloth. Vernon was graduating from public elementary school this year, or at least he was getting out. This year his grades had been awful. The elementary school was OK, but their public junior high was dangerous and gang-ridden. The kid was going through an awful stage. He'd put himself between a rock and a hard place, and he knew it. He'd pushed his dinner plate out into the center of the table—because who on earth, really, could be expected to eat that stuff?—and put his head down on the table, his face away from Philip.

Blam!

Vernon brought the flat of his hand down on the table as hard as he (presumably) could. The china—Haviland from Felicia's mother—jumped. The wineglasses jumped.

Blam!

Felicia covered her eyes with her hands. She seemed deep in her own thoughts. Vernon shifted in his chair, brought his face closer to a glass.

Blam!

"Vernon," his dad said, "what do you think you're doing?"

"Do something about it, Phil!" Felicia said.

Phil said, as mildly as he could, "I'm just asking him what he was doing. I mean, what is the impetus behind his acts? Is it an experiment of some kind?"

Blam!

The glasses jolted. Phil hastily snatched up his wine and drank it off.

"Vern," he said, "how's school?"

"Sucks," Vernon said, without lifting his head from the table.

"*Sucks* rhymes with *fucks*," Eloise remarked.

"I don't like that language at my table, Eloise," Phil said. "And Vern, you'd better begin paying attention in school, or you're going to find yourself someplace that won't be the kind of picnic you're used to."

"Don't care."

"What did you say?"

"Don't CARE!"

His sister smiled. "Maybe you'll get raped. *Sucks* rhymes with *fucks*."

"Eloise!" Felicia said. "Please."

Vernon brought his hand, palm down, onto the table with a terrific crash. Two water glasses crashed over and the last of the wine.

"Goddamn it," Philip said, "that's it! That was a hundred-dollar bottle of wine when I bought it five years ago. There's at least twenty dollars' worth of wine right there on the table!" He knew he sounded like a crank, an old crank. But it was hell to be responsible for three—what else could he call them?—leeches! Why couldn't Felicia be the kind of woman who needed a career to fulfill herself? The concept of work of any kind was entirely foreign to her. They'd had help since the minute they were married, a never-ending stream of Spanish-speaking peasants, who stayed until they learned some English or couldn't take it anymore and left.

There was no way out for him. Felicia's brother was a divorce lawyer. And he himself was bad with math. He couldn't hide an asset if he tried.

"You *could* cut down on your collection," Felicia said. As if that would change anything.

He could have said, You drink as much as I do and you know it, or, Wine's my only comfort in this hellhole of a house, or, You might want to do more with *your* life than shop, or, It was a dark day in my life when you spread your legs for me; if I'd only been thinking more closely about cause and effect!

But it was useless. He had just one project now. Eloise would be all right. As disagreeable as she was, she knew what kind of world she lived in; she pulled the grades and did the sports and had a healthy love of money. Phil's pension would take care of Felicia if anything happened to him, and if she had to live in slightly reduced circumstances, that would be ultrafine with him.

Vernon was something else. Something had gone wrong there.

"Vern, I'm going into the den now. You and I have to talk."

But once he got Vern in there, he had trouble figuring out what to do next. He took his own favorite leather chair, close to the fireplace, with the best view of the television, a nice piece of cherrywood that looked like a cupboard until you pressed a button and with a terrible groan the television heaved out. (He prudently kept hold of the remote so that Vern couldn't blow him off altogether.)

"Son," he said. "Son."

Phil's real dad had been a scholar, a professor, a man of taste who died too young. His stepdad was a man's man, respected by all, kind to his family. Always there in an emergency. He wanted to run his own life on both models, to be an honorable, professional family man, to take his kids both to museums and baseball games. Eloise sometimes went on jaunts with him because she knew which side her bread was buttered on. Or to get some fresh air. Or for an assignment from school. Since last year, she had passed on all that.

"Son," Phil said, and took a breath.

Vernon slumped in the couch, his knees apart, hunched his shoulders, and looked at the floor. He was so small for his age. Scrawny.

"Leaving the fifth grade is a very important time for any boy. You could say the time of childhood is past. You have to think about becoming a man . . ."

Vernon sighed.

" . . . whether you like it or not. It's not just a question of grades. Your report cards have not been good lately. Or your behavior."

Vernon rolled his eyes.

"You're one of only six in your class who haven't been recommended by the faculty for a private middle school. You know that, don't you? And two of those six are Special kids. You've got to shape up, Vern! Before it's too late. I'm not kidding. I'm not kidding about this. Vern?"

Vernon shrugged.

"I *mean* it!" He could hear his voice rising. "It's not too late. You can still redeem yourself. Isn't there anything you're good at? Something to concentrate on to raise your grade average, something you like?"

Silence.

"What about French? Your teacher said you could probably do much better if you'd only apply yourself. He said you had a real talent there, a natural talent with languages—"

"Silly-ass faggot!"

"*What* did you say?"

"Nothing."

"Math? Science? Gym?"

His son grunted.

Not for the first time, Phil considered that his son needed Ritalin or Zoloft, something to take the edge off.

"The thing is, if you don't get into a good middle school, you won't get into a good high school and you'll never get into a good university. We've been over this a thousand times, Vernon!"

"You work at UCLA," Vern said.

"Excuse me?"

"I said, you work at UCLA. You'll be able to get me in."

"Oh, Vern! It doesn't work that way. You've got to pull the grades. You've got to ace the SATs. You've got to succeed—"

He was going to say, *on your own merit*. But he was looking at the possibility that maybe the kid had lost his merit somehow. Maybe he would go to public schools and deal drugs if he was lucky, but Eloise might be right too. He'd probably get mugged or raped or half drowned in a toilet that wasn't even cleaned regularly. He'd have no skills. He wouldn't go to college and he'd end up working as a box boy. Or at Blockbuster, where he'd get raped and mugged again. Would Eloise take care of her brother when they got older? Not a chance. Eloise wouldn't pull her own mother out of a shallow pond.

Phil looked bleakly at the long years opening up in front of him. He had dreamed of putting their two children through good schools and then, at some point, selling the Santa Monica house for a healthy profit, cashing in his UCLA pension, and moving with Felicia to the south of France. Ryeres. La Ciotat. He had loved those towns when he was a student himself, bicycling, hitch-hiking, beginning to learn the different textures of wine, starting at the very bottom—harsh red almost-vinegar siphoned straight from a shopkeeper's barrel into the corked green bottle he'd kept in the basket of his bike at all times. He remembered the first Châteauneuf-du-Pape he'd bought with an unexpected check from home. And his first Lacryma Christi. *"Qui a fait si bonne cuisine?"* the lady at the youth hostel had said that night, when some kids were cooking. And he'd brought out his bottle.

Now—or soon, when the kids were gone and if the world didn't blow up—he knew exactly the place he wanted himself and Felicia to end their days. A stone cottage with thick walls and a kitchen garden and some two- or three-star restaurants close enough to drive to. And to be there when the Beaujolais Nouveau really was nouveau.

But he couldn't do it if Vernon was going to take this route he seemed to have decided on.

"Look. We're going out to interviews in the next couple of months. Your mom and I will do everything we can. We'll say the teachers had it in for you. We'll say you were too smart for the curriculum—that you were bored. That's true enough, isn't it?"

Vernon's eyes met his, like a housefly's, then flicked away.

"We'll say your social skills are below par because you're a genius in math. . . ."

Again Vernon looked at him. "Flunking math."

"Some science they haven't thought up yet! Pay attention, Vern! All you have to do is look presentable. You *come* from a good family; your sister's doing all right. We can get through this. This is just one of many steps, some of them hard, some of them easy, that lead to—"

He stopped. He couldn't stand to listen to himself.

"Hey, Eloise!" he yelled. "Felicia! Come on in here and let's watch television."

Mercifully, they came in. Felicia stretched out along the couch where she could touch Eloise if she wanted to, if Eloise would stand for it. Vernon found the hassock and pulled it up to where he almost blocked the set. Philip stabbed the remote, and the cherrywood cupboard gave its comforting groan as the screen rolled up.

"Any games on?"

"Nah."

They settled on yet another cop show where the men talked tough and the female police dressed like hookers. During a commercial, Phil went into the old-fashioned bar they'd put in under the den stairwell. It was dark in there, and paneled, and Phil could have stayed there happily for a week, with the Dutch door closed behind him, some good-quality crystal glasses, and more than enough good wine. His own private tastings. He opened a bottle and said, out into the den, "Want some, honey?"

Something must have happened to put her in a better mood, for she said, "Yes, please," and then, "Oh, look!"

He ducked out into the den and read, in one of those crawls they had at the bottom of almost every television channel these days, FOUR SUSPECTED TERRORISTS CAPTURED ON THE GROUNDS OF SAN ONOFRE NUCLEAR PLANT. ALL REPORTS OF POSSIBLE RADIO-ACTIVE LEAKS DENIED.

"Dad, is that close to us?" Vernon asked.

"Right on the road to San Diego," Eloise said. "Near the zoo. Where *you* belong."

"No. It's far away. Far enough away." But he made a note to get some potassium pills tomorrow at the hospital, if there were any left.

He backed out of the Meadow Oaks parking lot perhaps a little too fast, Vern slumped beside him in the passenger seat. It hadn't gone well, the interview. Now, in the car, neither one of them talked. Phil didn't trust himself to say anything. They swerved down Sunset Boulevard to Gelson's in the Palisades. The last time he'd picked up berries for Felicia he'd made the mistake of going to Ralph's and she'd clucked her tongue at them. *She'd clucked her tongue!* So he went to Gelson's and picked up salmon and black-berries and celery remoulade and a good bottle of wine and a peach cobbler, getting exactly what he wanted, for a change, while Vern tagged along, being the person who wasn't being spoken to, although the thing with him was you could not speak to him for two months and he probably wouldn't notice.

Phil paid and they went out past the security guard and he got to see once again the squadrons of women who—as far as he could see—had never done a day's real work in their lives, and their pampered children, dull-eyed, waiting to be hauled to their next lesson in whatever. It really was too much: lives wasted, his own life sucked away. He slammed the groceries into the back of his car, climbed in, and, without waiting for Vernon to fasten his seat belt, put the Lexus in reverse. And hit something.

They surrounded his car, a dark-skinned family—not Mexican—shouting.

"We kept signaling! Couldn't you see us signal? Didn't you hear us honk? Get out of the car! Look at that damage! What's your insurance? We demand to see your license!"

It was a woman, heavyset, unusual for this part of town, with three kids. She wore a floppy sweater and a long full skirt. A little girl in a red dress with a bad cold had set up a horrid screeching wail. A boy about twelve, in old clothes, held his head and groaned, while a scrawny adolescent guy, maybe sixteen, pounded on Vern's door and kept repeating, "Get out of the *car*! Take a look at what you've *done*! You hurt my ma! Get out of the car, take a look, get out of the *car*!"

Instead, Phil took a look around for the security guard. He could see him, over by the entrance to the store, closely supervising the parking of a harmless bakery truck. You couldn't blame the guy for not coming over. Everybody was afraid now, of everything. Anybody could be armed, or have a bomb. Or a disease. Or all three.

"Get out of the car!" It was the woman yelling now. "Look what you've done!"

Over on Vernon's side the sixteen-year-old was still pounding on the door. Phil could see and hear the little girl wailing. Well-dressed wives scurried past, staying away, out of trouble. The heavyset woman's face was twisted with rage.

"All right, all right!" He stepped out of the car and went around to the back to look at the damage to his own car first.

"I don't see anything."

"Of *course*! Your big truck thing is so big you run right over honest citizens. People like you don't care! You *look* at that! How could you, when I was signaling and everything."

People put up a fuss about gas-guzzling SUVs, but her car was in its way just as big, a Buick or a Chevy Malibu with many dents, a bashed-in front end, and a crumpled bumper with just about every color of the rainbow on it.

"Look what you've *done*!" she howled.

"I don't think I did that. Because, look, there's no damage to my car at all."

"My head feels like it's going to fall off, Mama," the middle boy said. "I think I have to go to the hospital."

"Get out of the car, you little runt!" the teenager yelled at Vern. Phil noticed the kid's T-shirt was dirty and torn.

"Stay right there," he shouted to his son. "You stay out of this!"

"*There,* right *there*!" the heavyset woman announced, and pointed to a fleck of red on the bumper. "You can't deny it. Shame on you! This man," she began to scream at passersby, "he's trying to rob me because I'm not rich! I demand to see his license! I demand to see his insurance!"

Because he'd been told this all his life, and because it was the right thing to do, Phil reached in his wallet for his driver's license. She snatched it from him, held it close to his face, looked at him suspiciously, then gave it to her middle boy.

"Write everything down," she said. "Then get his insurance."

"May I see *your* license?"

The little girl set up a howl and began to blow her nose on her skirt. He noticed, sadly, that her cotton panties were dirty, loose fitting, and worn.

Fuck it, he thought, I can take the hit, and moved toward the passenger side of the SUV, where the teenager was still slapping on the window.

"Get out of the way," he said, "so I can get to my glove compartment."

He had to push the kid behind him so he could open the door. As he reached in, or began to reach in, Vern slid out underneath him and went for the teenager. His head only came up to the guy's ribs, so he went for him there, butting him as hard as he could.

"Fucking ass-bite faggot! Stay away from my dad!" Vern's thick hands reached up and grabbed the kid's ears and yanked him down. He butted his head hard against the kid's head and then kneed him in the crotch. The guy knelt on the ground between cars, groaning.

The woman and the daughter were both crying now, genuine tears. Vern went for the middle kid and punched him in the face. Blood poured from his nose, onto Gelson's parking lot.

"Give me my dad's license, faggot ass-bite! Give it to me *now,* unless you want what your brother got! Dad! Get in the car and *start* it!"

Phil and the heavyset woman looked at each other. *Kids,* their looks said momentarily.

Then her eyes filled with hate and shiftiness and he heard the sound of Vern's fists against flesh again and he knew enough to get in the car and start it. He backed out of his place, slowly and carefully, making sure to miss the retching teenager, trusting all the others to look out for themselves. He reached over and opened the passenger-seat door. Vern jumped in, clutching the driver's license, which was drenched in blood.

"Fasten your seat belt," Phil said.

They stopped at a Starbucks a few blocks away, and Vernon went in to clean up. They ordered Frappuccinos.

Phil said, "They must have been, you know, like the people who do that in parking lots? For insurance money? Gypsies?"

"Goddamn Arabs is what they were."

"Watch your language. Every bad person isn't an Arab."

The place was filling up by now, a Wednesday afternoon around three thirty or four in Pacific Palisades: mothers, and sometimes dads, coming in with their kids for a treat after school. If any place in the world is safe, this is safe, Phil thought, watching the dust motes in the afternoon sunlight; the other stuff is just on television. He thought of San Onofre, eighty miles away, of all the dubious unmarked targets all over the city and state that made nuclear weapons or their components. A kid on a board skated by, debonair, dodging outdoor tables, beautifully impervious. People could die, Phil thought. Every one of us is going to die, in fact.

He said, "You did good, Vern."

The boy flicked a glance at him, looked away, took a swallow of Frappuccino that left icy foam on his lips, then looked at his hands, which were puffed and bleeding. He smiled.

"What'll we tell your mom?"

Vern shrugged.

But Felicia was so deep into her own world that she only asked, "What did you do with this salmon? How come it isn't still cold?" And then, apprehensively, "How was the interview?"

"Fine," Phil said. "Vernon did fine."

"We had some fun," Vern said. And went upstairs.

PHIL

"I want another baby. Maybe two."

He heard her but it didn't register. They were propped up in bed watching another police drama on television, and he'd been looking at his father's hands lying slackly on the coverlet—duvet, whatever they called them now. Good slim-fingered hands, very competent looking, their wrists covered by his pajamas. How weird was that? His father's hands.

"Phil? Please. Listen to me."

"I'm right here."

But he was a thousand miles away. Dad was reading him the funnies, turning the pages with his elegant, slim hands. Before he died. He did that sometimes.

"I know there are arguments against it. The world situation. The terrorists. All that business. I know we have the two, but there's another whole side to it."

She had his attention now.

"And I know we've talked about my sometime going to work. But the thing is—"

"What? *What?*"

"I don't want to. Because—"

"What?"

"I don't want to."

"For God's *sake,* Felicia!"

"You do what *you* want to," she said defiantly. The light came from behind her head, onto her softening chin, the thin down beginning on her cheek.

"What do you mean?" He breathed harder, felt himself blushing.

"Go off every day. Do important things. Be the center of attention. Play tennis. Eat all your rich food. See your friends."

"They're your friends too."

"They're not."

"They are. They are."

He hated the way she looked at him, like he was some kind of donkey. Like he would never, in ten worlds, *get* it.

"Dr. and Mrs.," she said.

"Well? So?"

"You've got everything your way."

If you only knew, he wanted to cry out, but it wouldn't be kind.

What do you mean? he thought of asking her again, but what if she knew something he didn't want her to know?

"You do. I don't have anything. I just don't have anything. I see the future and I'm—I'm not looking forward to it. There's nothing for me."

"But you have—" He was going to say, *You have everything you want.* Something his stepdad would have said, did say, to his mother sometimes. Something made him go on. "Two nice kids, the house you said you wanted. This was your idea." (Unspoken: *All this was your idea.*) He sounded like a husband out of the comics. Dagwood.

"If I went back to work, what would I do? I don't want to do it!"

"So stay home!"

Here came the tears. "*You*'ve always got a project. Somebody's always sick. Someone's always going to get better. Or worse. Every morning you've got something to do."

"Well, I—"

"Four walls. Four *walls*! That's what I have. All I have. That's what this is. You get up; you go away. Eloise goes away. Vernon goes away. Nobody talks to me. There's no one to talk to."

"But that's life, isn't it? Isn't life like that for everybody? You have your friends. We have a good life. Nobody gets to—"

"It would keep me young. To have another baby."

Pity killed him, just killed him. *In your dreams,* he thought.

"Because the kids don't talk to us anymore. That's normal, I know. But you know what? It would give us ten more years to be a family. Eleven, if you count me being pregnant. Twelve. They don't get awful until then. Maybe thirteen."

"We'd be in our late fifties."

"But then we wouldn't have to worry about it. Because we'd be in our fifties!"

"God."

"I need somebody to love me," she said bitterly.

"I love you. You know I love you," he said.

She didn't bother to answer.

"No, I do. I *do,* really. What makes you think I don't?"

Don't you think this world-situation thing is a little out of *control*? That's what he wanted to say. He wanted to say, Do you think we both don't know Eloise is sneaking out at night? Don't you know I fool around sometimes? Don't we both know that something's up with Vernon, something's *really* up? So isn't the whole thing a fiasco by now? But you're decent and I'm decent so there's nothing to be done about it. We have to ride it out. At least until the kids are grown.

Which is when it hit him. Thirteen more years. Twenty-three more years. His whole life, that's what she wanted.

"Poor kid," he said. "Poor Felicia."

She turned her head down and away.

"I'm sorry. I'm so sorry."

She didn't answer. She sniffed. "Forget it," she said. "Just forget it." Then, "If we can't have more kids, can we just get out of here? Buy a farm in Connecticut? So I'd have something to *do*?"

"There's something up with Vern," he said.

"If you were home more. If you cared at all about your family!" It was automatic, just a dance step.

"I *am* home. I'm home all the time. I'm making the effort. I'm *home*. But we ought to—"

"He's a *monster*, Phil. And you just let it go. Like you do everything. He treats me like dirt when you're not here."

"And you want *more* kids?"

She turned away from him and began to cry. "Can't you see?" she wept. "Can't you see *anything*?"

Now, tonight, and every night of my life, he thought. This is it. And then I'll die. But first I'll be sick. I'll lose my teeth. My jaw will keep dropping open, even when I'm awake. I'll break my hip. Eloise will keep giving me those looks. Felicia will sigh. I'll slop milk on the kitchen floor like Charlie. I'll wear pajama tops and sweatpants and then I'll die. Here on the Westside. At Saint John's. Or Santa Monica Hospital. Or at UCLA. Or at home like Charlie. Or we'll all go up at once from some bomb.

"You're such a perfectionist! Your swordfish is too done! The hollandaise doesn't have enough lemon! But you completely overlook his behavior. Oh, you talk! But you don't *do* anything. He gets away with murder!"

It was one of those things they both knew. Phil was the one who loved Vernon.

With a terrible, soft, embarrassing love.

So now he was the one who said, "Forget it. Just stop, can't you?"

The horrible rape on the television had been solved. Now the news began: another blown-up bus, somewhere in the Middle East, untidy bodies strewn across a dirt road. He reached for the remote, and Felicia twisted over to the far side of the bed, deep into her *don't touch me* mode, as if he wanted to right now.

"Could we go to Australia then?" Her voice floated out into the room, high and taut. "Can't we do anything at all? Buy an avocado farm?"

He turned off the television. She got like this sometimes: fritzy. You just had to ride it out.

PHIL

He couldn't find it at first. He drove up and down Wilshire from the beach back to Twenty-sixth or so, glancing every once in a while at the newspaper ad beside him—a full-page one, with pictures of high school grads who had been accepted by some very dubious colleges, like Coulter or Lewis and Clark. The message, very clear: Look! They graduated! They're faking their way into the adult community *some* way or other, and *we* did it!

He didn't even know if the school started in sixth grade, but it was worth a try. And he wouldn't waste time on why Felicia wasn't doing this. She wasn't, so she wasn't.

He turned around at Twenty-sixth, headed back west. Slowly. There it was, in a second-story office building setup: Evergreen

High School. Underground parking, an elevator. A receptionist. A couple of classrooms with four or five burned-out-looking kids; you could see them through windows opening onto the hall. And, at the end of the hall, the headmaster's office with the headmaster in it.

Phil leaned across the desk to shake hands; the guy—balding and wearing a bad suit—didn't bother to get up. Because if you had to come here, you were already on your knees.

"Why don't you tell me all about it?" the headmaster suggested.

"It's my son. He's going into the sixth grade. Vernon is a pretty special kid. I don't mean special *needs,* I mean he's . . ."

He went on, trying to explain—without begging—that Vern was different but great. How he got bored easily. Had an inquiring mind. Liked to figure out how things worked. Had a really astonishing gift for languages. How his grades had gone down drastically this year, but it was just a stage. But he got straight A's in French. He got a little truculent at times, but he'd never done anything to harm anyone, ever! Yes, certainly, he was *different,* not average in any way. His main problem was his refusal to *go along to get along*—waving fingers in the air to illustrate what he meant—he didn't even give you a smile unless he really *meant* to give you a smile.

"I imagine you've applied to other private schools here in town? What was their take on . . . Vernon?"

"His grades aren't good enough. Or maybe I'm not rich enough. Or poor enough. He doesn't qualify for a scholarship.

And I'm not a producer, I'm a doctor! Frankly, I don't know. I don't know!"

"Our tuition is high, higher than Crossroads, higher than Meadow Oaks, but we offer a one-in-four teaching ratio. I imagine you saw some of that when you came in. However, we're full up. You should have come to us earlier in the school year."

There was a little touch of Vernon in the guy's tone. Payback. For what? For being stuck in the creepiest school for the creepiest possible kids? Payback to proud parents who got stuck with a lemon?

"Look. Like I said, I'm a doctor. I'm prepared, like any parent, to do my share for the school. I'd be happy to do it. You probably need somebody to come in and—I don't know—be the doctor on career day. Give a lecture on AIDS or abstinence or birth control—"

"We have teachers for that."

"Well, how about basketball? Or track? Like, you could use someone to—hang out with the kids. Not chaperone them exactly, but *hang out*! Be a role model."

He saw in the headmaster's face that if Phil had been such a good role model he wouldn't be here now, in this position.

"Look," he went on miserably, "I could arrange for tours, small student tours, to the UCLA Medical Center where I work. Expand their notions, maybe, of what they can do when they graduate." As if any of those morons could ever make it to UCLA, even at the undergraduate level, except as a groundskeeper. But what did he know? Maybe they were all fine. Just misunderstood. Like Vern.

"You're over at UCLA?"

"Yes."

"What's your field?"

"Dermatology. Why?" He wondered where this was going.

"You're going to have to do something for me. To make it worth my while. We have a woman on the faculty who's been on the kidney wait list for a long time. We have a couple of people here with pretty bad arthritis who have an Oxycontin habit. Or Vicodin. Even some who can't afford insurance. They don't get paid much here. Free office visits would be a big help. And prescriptions."

Phil felt dizzy. "I can't do that, any of it! You know the kinds of chances I'd be taking? I'm not going to break the law to get my son in your school! I could . . . I could go to the police about this. It's unconscionable!"

The headmaster heard him out. "You could, but you won't. It's a he-said / he-said situation. I haven't done anything but talk. Santa Monica High has had four shootings this year. Venice High is gangland city. I understand your need to get your boy into a private middle school. I hear you saying he has problems. Believe me, I hear you! We see these kids all the time. I know, down to the head, how many openings there are in private schools on the Westside and in the Valley. Right now there's not room for even one more bad apple. Of course you can always send him to New Mexico or Arizona—wilderness school, one of those places. But it's expensive and it's brutal. It doesn't sound to me like you want that. Or you can end up sending him to Samohi and let him take his chances. People do it all the time."

"You're actually telling me—"

"What makes you think *you're* entitled?" the headmaster said suddenly. "I get parents in here every few days. They've exhausted their possibilities or they wouldn't be here. They do what it takes to get their kids in. Whatever it is. Or they don't! It's not my problem. You get that?"

"What you suggest," Phil said stiffly, "is absolutely out of the question. Never. Not me."

"We're finished, then."

After that, there really wasn't much to do but get up, turn around, go out past those small classes, and push the elevator *down*.

There had to be something else, something he could do. He saw Vern in his mind's eye, alone on a gang-ridden playground or shoved up against a locker by some guy with tattoos. "Absolutely out of the question," he repeated out loud, after he got in the car. "Not my son!"

EDITH

"So what is it again with your son and you?" Melinda asked me during one long afternoon. "You seem a little . . . I don't know, tough on him? He seems like such a nice man."

"He just—he *just can't help himself,* you know? Let me give you an example. There's a housecoat made of toweling that I always liked. I had it a long time, before he was born. I wore it at home, during the day, when I was alone. Ordinarily, I'm very careful of my appearance. Or careful enough. *You* know. But one time he barged in through the front door (he's always done that; my place is still home to him, or at least he thinks so), and caught me in that robe with my hair in those curlers we used to wear, and he said, 'Making a fashion statement?' He's what we used to call a wiseacre. Sometimes he rubs me the wrong way, is all."

We went back to silence and I thought of what I couldn't say. That once a niece of mine went home to see her mother, my half-sister, in the middle of the day (she said she'd been calling there for two days and hadn't gotten an answer), and she did the same thing; she barged in the front door using her own key, and, according to her story, her mother and her father were both dead asleep—passed out, that would be—surrounded by empty beer cans and empty bottles of vodka, and out in the kitchen the sink was filled with dirty dishes and old dead food and flies all over everything and of course, according to my niece, she thought they were dead, each in their separate Barcaloungers, and did she call the morgue? No, she called Phil.

They went right to it, Phil and my niece, picking up the cans and opening the windows and running the vacuum after Phil made sure they were alive. But her parents weren't fit to live alone! That was the position Phil and my niece took. When my half-sister sobered up, or came to, or whatever it was, she invited them to leave but they turned down the invitation. They gave her an ultimatum (they call it an intervention now). They said it was rehab or a nursing home. Because Mom and Dad obviously "couldn't take care of themselves."

Or there was the time Phil barged right in, as usual, in the middle of the day, and Pierre was there, giving me a massage. I much prefer a massage at home. I don't much like going down to Burke Williams and soaking in a tub with a lot of twenty-year-olds and then, just for instance, getting whapped with wet mops by Japanese masseuses or sponged down with milk or something equally silly, because let's get real, let's get real for a minute! When you get a massage you want to be touched!

I've listened to women say they've joined Alanon when they've never even known a drunk, because what they need is proximity to a human being, preferably with a dick. I've known women to say they were crazy, or at the very least depressed, and pony up a hundred and seventy dollars an hour, for as long as they could afford it, for the privilege and opportunity of pouring out their hearts to some stone-faced bully across the room. Just to be in some guy's company.

I preferred Pierre, a nice old French guy who brought his own table with him and came over to the house, and I pulled the shades and lay on his table in my chaste cotton underwear and for ninety minutes he touched me. Not the way you might think! Just touching. His conversation was all about fruits and vegetables; he was very high on something called a "liver flush," castor oil and lemon juice taken three times a day, which he said would fix any-thing. He didn't nag me, though. He was fond of saying, "I am not a fan-ah-teek!" And he wasn't. And one afternoon about three in the afternoon, with the shades down and Pierre in his second hour of work, in barges Phil, takes one look at his almost naked mother, and bellows like a bison, *What the hell is going on here?* Poor Pierre never came back.

And then there was the time when I took myself out to dinner—I was getting quite good at it—and had a dozen oysters and three martinis; I was reading a good book, I don't see why women say it's hard to go out alone, it's not, really.

I came home and took an Ambien, turned on the television to watch the awful news, and went to sleep. I woke up in the night and took another one or two. I don't like to be awake at night. And woke up at four in the afternoon with the sun in my eyes and Phil shaking me. "I've been trying to reach you all day! You've got to have a job! You've got to stop *doing* this, or I'm going to have to do something myself!"

"What?" I said. "What?"

I was looking at his poor sweet face when he said—at least my awful niece wasn't there for this—"Can't you find a way to, I don't know, *volunteer your time*?"

Which is how I ended up here, in the waiting room of the UCLA Medical Center. And why Phil, from either shyness or shame, usually finds a way to come to work through one of the side doors.

"My love life sucks, by the way," I told Melinda, to cheer her up.

A couple of weeks ago some guy called. At first, I didn't recognize the voice.

"Becky's husband? I was married to Becky?"

"Oh! Sure! How are you?" Becky'd been dead about a year.

"Is it raining over there too?"

"Yes. Cats and dogs."

The glamour of it all.

"So this morning I asked myself what I should do, and I said, I know. I'll call up Edith and ask her out."

"Why, that's nice!"

"I thought you might"—his voice began to fade—"like to go listen to some jazz?"

After we got off the phone, I tried to remember. What did he look like? I'd known him for years, but what did he look like?

He showed up in that standard black leather and a pale green shirt, but those stylish duds didn't seem to match his face. On the other hand, I couldn't seem to look him in the face. Which was crazy, because I'd known him for years.

I began to talk—I had such bad small talk anymore—about my son and grandchildren, as if anybody cared. About the government and how berserk it was. About the war. About the draft and if my grandson would get caught in it.

"It'll be going on for years."

"I'm sorry?"

"The war. For years."

He asked me a few jazz questions then, testing questions. Who had I seen? Who had I ever seen?

"Fats Waller? Back in the fifties? My mother took me when I was a little girl. At a place on Hollywood Boulevard?"

He didn't believe me. But I remembered being there, and Mr. Waller singing "Two Sleepy People," and even what I wore.

"Art Pepper? Over at the Haig? My mother sneaked me in. I only saw him the one time. He was playing with Gerry Mulligan. And Chet Baker, of course."

"Who else?"

"What?"

"Who else was in the *group*?" Because anybody would know Gerry Mulligan and Chet Baker.

"Bob Whitlock?"

Did his hands relax the tiniest bit on the steering wheel? He didn't press me further and I was glad, because I couldn't remember whether Bob Whitlock had been on drums or bass.

But it was wonderful, once we got to the Jazz Bakery, and there were more people in black leather, drifting around in a foyer, drinking white wine from plastic glasses, the audience divided equally or almost equally between really little kids from high school, white and black, shepherded by fanatical high school teachers who loved jazz, and really old hipsters who all seemed to know one another.

"I've followed Big J across the country," a brassy old bat with dyed blond hair and a spandex bodysuit said to me in the restroom, "and I'd do it again."

"Cannonball's going to be here next week. You coming?"

"Wouldn't miss it!"

Four performers came out, one by one, really old guys in glossy, well-pressed suits of brown or tan gabardine, wearing well-shined, cracked, pointy-toed leather shoes. They wore ties, French cuffs. The drummer was a white guy, in his twenties, wearing a sweatshirt.

They played an old riff, "There Will Never Be Another You." The audience sighed, one long sigh of recognition and the anticipation of bliss. How could these guys be so beautiful, so great, so delicious?

They broke off to do solos, the tenor and then the alto, the tenor again, then the alto, then looked over to the piano, where the guy did something amazing and virtuosic, if that was the word, and I took the time to look around. My date's knees were beating double-time, his face a mask of pure pleasure. All around me, hipsters were moving their heads in hypnotized time-bound nods, going *no, no, no, no, no.* They knew when the solos would end; they counted the bars and began their applause a bare beat before each solo ended. The horn players stepped back, just a baby step, as their music finished.

Then they came back together for the final riff, the unsung words:

There may be other lips that I may kiss . . .
but there will never be another you. . . .

We ate in the restaurant next door, a pretty place but not terribly fancy, a bistro with duck breast and decent champagne. We began to have a good time.

"Edith! Is that *you*?" I looked up from the table to see Marina Bokelman, an old friend, decked out in scarves and costume jewelry and freshly hennaed hair. She looked great and had a man in tow. "This is my friend Steve Knox. We're down from Grass Valley. Wasn't that music *something*? Steve, this is my old friend Edith. We've known each other from graduate school. Isn't it amazing to find you here?"

I looked across the table at the man I'd come with. There was no way in hell I knew what his name was.

He never called back.

"It's really tiresome to be alone," I said to Melinda, and then I could have smacked myself. She was looking at the same damn thing, a husband on dialysis with who knew how much time to live.

PHIL

He knew the way by more than heart: the turn off Wilshire into Westwood and left by the campus to the medical center parking entrance and the basement entrance after that, up the long inspiring walk to what was, really, one of the finest teaching hospitals in the nation. On automatic he walked through the great waiting room, nodded to his mom, turned right, took the elevator to the fourth floor, turned left, turned right, and right again into the back door of his—quite nice—office.

From there he went out to reception and sneaked up on Kathi and poked her between the shoulder blades. She would sigh and say, "Good morning, doctor." Sometimes she'd jump and blurt out, "You!" Or she might say, even with patients in the waiting room, "Grow up, Phil," or "Give it a rest, can't you?" But he didn't give it a rest. Why should he?

He knew most guys did their rounds before eight in the morning, but what the hell. He wasn't a big-time surgeon; in academic terms he'd never get beyond associate professor. He scheduled most of his appointments from nine to twelve, and generally speaking he didn't have anyone to make rounds to anyway. Sometimes a foot fungus would get out of hand, or some poor woman with infected mosquito bites from her last Mexican cruise would have stumbled on to him by mistake. But he went for the less stress the better. He loved the easy cases.

He got in early this morning and, after he'd changed into his white jacket, went out the same back door he'd come in. He turned toward what he thought was north—close to the physical science buildings—and lost his bearings at once.

He came up on a glass wall with a set of babies beyond it, turned in embarrassment and barged off in another direction, got on an elevator and went two floors up, realized that everybody here was dying—probably of cancer—and took the elevator down again. Were people looking at him? He fumbled for his name tag and, when he got off the elevator, took it off and put it in his pocket.

ICU. NO ADMITTANCE EXCEPT FOR FAMILY. This wasn't it. His heart was beating hard enough to feel.

"May I help you, doctor?" A teenage volunteer in pink scrubs looked sweetly at him.

"Ah, no." He turned and started to walk. Of course she knew he was a doctor because of—not because of the laminated identification card that hung from his neck by a plastic cord, with a bad picture of him plastered all over it. He bent his head, took a look at his tag, then turned it over. Kept his hand over it. Found an elevator. Took it down to the main floor, past the information desk, the florist shop, the gift shop, his mom, gave her an uneasy wave. He found the medical directory, stood gawking at it like any other rube with a bad heart or a stomachache. He was terrible at this. He remembered that time, back in the day, when he actually had written out a couple of triplicate prescriptions for medical cocaine so that he and Felicia could get high. The second time—just the second time he did it—a senior member of the staff followed him out of the hospital pharmacy and said two words: "No more."

"May I help you, doctor?" It was another young volunteer.

"No! Uh. Maybe." He blushed. Blood rang in his ears. I could have a stroke, he thought. I'm not too young for one.

"I'm wondering." The word for kidney specialist or the field of sick kidneys entirely left him. "I'm looking for—dialysis? Kidney dialysis? Uh, apheresis?"

She looked at him with curiosity.

"I'm trying to get to *know* the rest of the hospital! Giving myself a tour! It's . . . like we don't get to know the place we're working out of! And it's possible that I—"

His mother looked down at the blotter on her desk. Thinking, probably, why hadn't he asked her? It's what she was there for.

"Seventh floor to your right. And there's an adjunct facility down in Westwood."

He took the elevator again, forced himself to walk slowly, remove his hand from his name tag. He passed a nurses' station and a couple of other alcoves with computers and phone banks. He got to a door marked DIALYSIS. Looked at it. Opened it.

Just another gorgeous UCLA Med Center room. Long and wide, no windows, maybe twelve recliners with people in them, all looking fixedly at television sets dangling in front of them from the ceiling. The walls were banked with machines.

"May I help you?"

Another volunteer, this one ten years older than God.

But he felt a little better now.

"You know," he said, "sometimes we get so caught up in our own specialties that we forget about the larger field of medicine. I'm just making the rounds—between *my* rounds. . . ."

She eyed him. "I'm sure that's very nice. But there's not much to see."

"They look very comfortable."

"It's not a painful procedure."

"What's the prognosis? I mean, generally speaking."

"That really wouldn't be for me to say. Some of these patients have become my friends over the years."

"The . . . waiting list. Is that, by chance, accessible to the layman? The public?"

"Would you like some coffee, doctor? If you can wait a minute I'm sure I could get in touch with someone who can tell you. We have doughnuts, as you can see."

"No, thank you! I'll just be leaving then."

He double-timed it down the hall. Took the elevator down to

his own floor. Went in by the back way to his office. Went out to check in at the reception room. Kathi sat at the phone. "No, he *was* here, but he's stepped out. . . . I don't know. . . . No, no."

He knew he should go up and give her his usual poke, but he didn't have it in him. "I'm in, Kathi," he said, and went into his office and shut the door.

PHIL

It wasn't as though he had only his family to worry about. He had another woman, like everybody else. How it had happened was a little unclear to him.

He parked his car around the corner and kept his head down as he walked the block to her apartment. He knew it was silly. He didn't know anyone in these few blocks but her, but Babalu was up there on Montana, three quarters of a block away, and somebody he knew might want to eat Cuban. Or there could be a patient from any time, anywhere, who might recognize him. He could never keep track of them, and why should he? How could he?

So he bent his head down parallel to the sidewalk, and almost ran into an old man who didn't say *Watch where you're going* but could have, should have. Then there was the bamboo planting and the four steps down into the little cement enclosure, and he pressed the button for her apartment and kept his head down some more, because certainly every tenant in this place knew him by now and some even said hello when they saw him in the halls. And he waited for someone to say, *Didn't I see you once up at UCLA when I went in for my eczema? Didn't you misdiagnose my poison oak?*

But of course the cement enclosure and the modest lobby and the elevator with the false marbled sheeting were all empty, silent, tomblike. Almost sprinting, he got to her door, which was open slightly, and he wondered where she was because she'd just rung him in.

No one in the living room, or in the formal dining room she loved so much because she had a hutch crammed to its teeth with sterling silver, and he cringed to think of her poor husband, who'd worked himself to death to provide all this crap, the puffy couch covered with expensive gray silk, the fragile French straight chairs no human could sit on, the crystal chandelier hanging over the teak dining set. All this stuff piled into a two-bedroom apartment because her husband, after all that, had died and left her alone with next to nothing in the bank. Her children were out of school and could take care of themselves, thank God.

Sally's strategy was to hole up for now, with her linen napkins and her silver service and her modest inheritance, and wait for another Mr. Right to come by. She was still beautiful, she'd told him so herself, and contrary to popular belief, good wives—really good wives—were in short supply. All this from a simple blemish on her chin, a moment in his office when this slightly plump fortyish blonde perched on the crackly paper on the end of his examining table, crossing and recrossing her legs in their noisy pantyhose. She'd been all done up in white silk, in a bowed blouse that tied around her neck, and she'd patted her throat with fingernails tinted bloodred. "I don't know what's wrong," she'd said, "I don't know what's *wrong*! Does it continue into my mouth?" She collared her neck with her left hand, tilted her head back, and opened her lips. Her skin was amazingly elastic, her lipstick expertly applied, her mouth not open quite enough for him to see.

He should have said *Open wide, wider,* but his head suddenly weighed fifty pounds or more and he had to rest it against hers, had to insert his tongue into that pretty, sucking pink hole.

"Oh, oh!" she'd gasped, and moved her right leg up around his, even as his whole worried body began a tug-of-war with itself, his better half trying to get his head back in standing position, up between his shoulders, where he could get a decent look at whatever he was supposed to be looking at, and that other half, sinking, falling, rising, his mind blocked, fixated on a time when he'd taken the kids to the San Diego Zoo and they'd been high on a walkway in the aviary, and a pale green gecko had scuttled up to them, opened his mouth, and sung a love song, his throat pulsing and pink like this woman's mouth.

"Not here," he gasped. He was dizzy from surprise.

She reached up and ran her nails lightly across his left check. "Where, then? Where?"

Which was why, instead of going over to the Faculty Rec Center to play tennis from two to five in the afternoon with Jack

Josephson, half the time now he blew Jack off with a story about tennis elbow and drove away from UCLA like a bat out of hell, cutting through Westwood over to Veteran, then to Wilshire Boulevard, then down Montana, hyperventilating, terrified that Jack would call up Felicia one of these days and say, "Isn't Phil ever going to get that elbow of his taken care of?" Or Felicia herself would be out there, on Montana, buying boutique purses or God *knows* what, but he couldn't help it; that bright pink throbbing throat brought him out to the apartment on Eighth Street in Santa Monica a block down from Babalu, and for two—no, three—hours, maybe twice a week, he lost himself in this experience that he couldn't justify or figure out. His own brain yammered at him: Are you crazy? *Are you nuts?* What in God's name do you think you're doing? Everything you've worked for all these years, your career, your kids, your family could—no, it *will*—go down the drain and you'll be out on the street, unable to meet your responsibilities!

And he couldn't even hear that other voice, saying reassuringly, Men do this stuff all the time and nobody gets hurt. If the woman was going to some ethics committee, she would have done it long ago. The less I have sex with my wife the better she likes it. There's even the argument that I'm better with my kids because I'm not so tense all the time. Nobody ever got hurt by a few hours spent in the sack.

He never thought any of that. His mind went black as the inside of a cow and he fell on the woman, fell into her, drugged and useless, woke up for twenty minutes, listened to her chat about things, putting her life plan together. Then the doping, the anesthesia, would come over him again and in he'd sink. ("You do like conventional sex, don't you?" she'd said once. "So do I. I like to be filled up by a man, in the old sense. There's really nothing better.")

Usually she was there to meet him at the door, holding a couple of perfectly frosted gin martinis, dressed up in about twenty yards of green chiffon over a satin nightgown, with the blinds in the apartment drawn, but sometimes she waited for him in bed; he guessed that would be the way today. He ducked in there, his head already falling over again, bending down, ready to fall, to kiss, to sink, to forget. And there she was, in the bedroom's half-light, her blond hair all over the pillow, lace-edged sheets pulled up right under her chin. She worried about her double chin but he didn't; he loved it, it was satiny, silken.

"I can't do anything today, Phil. I'm glad you came over, but I can't do anything today."

"Why not?" He should have said, What's wrong, darling? but he thought about it too late. "What's wrong?" he added. "I hope nothing."

"I'm sick. Nothing serious. Just a little sick."

"Hey!" He pulled up an upholstered chair and put his hand to her brow. "Let's play doctor," he mumbled. "Like we always do." His head sank toward hers.

"No," she cried, "not today! I have the flu. That must be it. Every bone in my body aches. I thought about calling you but I know you hate that."

"Sick?" he said dumbly. "The flu? That's too bad. But you know, I can prescribe something. Let's take a look at you first."

"No!" she said.

She looked remarkably good for someone sick. Bending over her, he saw that her makeup had, as always, been carefully applied; he smelled the strong combination of perfume and hair spray. There was none of that mucusy flu breath, nothing sour about her. He reached to put his hand on her forehead again and she twitched away.

"My head is splitting!"

"I can prescribe something. Tamiflu. It'll shorten the length of the virus by two or three days." He was sitting on the bed now.

Her face altered in a way that reminded him of his wife's.

"Let me take a look at you," he said.

"No! Get away from me!"

"But Sally—"

He snatched the covers back, because it was good to be decisive. "I just need to see—"

She was fully clothed, in her best powder-blue Escada suit, yellow silk blouse, blue and yellow scarf, pantyhose, tan pumps. Looking like a million bucks.

"I'm going out," she explained, "a little later."

He stared at her.

"Don't look at me like that! I can go out if I want to!"

"But what—"

"You know that man who lives next to me, the CEO—I told you—and his wife has been dying of cancer? Actually, he doesn't live next to me now, but when my husband was still alive we . . . ran into each other several times. The poor man's heart was breaking. How could I say no? I gave my body to him out of generosity. It was very intense for both of us."

"Didn't you tell me she died?" he asked. He remembered the scene perfectly, he, lying exhausted, his head buried in the cave between her breast and plump upper arm, hearing her voice from far away as she told stories from a life he cared absolutely nothing about.

"He was heartbroken, of course, when she passed on. I wrote him notes. The shock was very deep. He waited six months before he got in touch with me. His sense of propriety is very strong. He told me he knew he should have waited the full year but he's obsessed with me, Philip! He says he's never known a love like this before."

"So, you're going out? With *him*?"

"We meet in secret." Her fingers nervously pulled her skirt closer to her knees. "His sons and daughters are terribly jealous. I think they're worried about their inheritance! I understand his doubts and feelings. His home is sacred to the memory of his wife and marriage. They were together thirty-eight years. His children would be terribly upset to see him in love again, so soon and so completely."

"Where do you go?"

"The Bel Air Hotel. He takes a suite. Or at least he *will* be doing that. Under an assumed name. He's very well known in this city. We have to be careful."

"You go to the *Bel Air*? You call that hiding out?"

"It's a temporary thing. We'll be married when the year is out."

"How do you know?"

"I know. That's all, Philip."

They looked at each other. "He must be twenty years older than you, at least."

"Twenty-seven."

But *you* aren't that young, he thought. You're older than I am, I know it for a fact. He realized, dimly and too late, that she might favor classically tailored clothes to discipline her soft, lax body.

"Listen," he said. "Can't we do it one last time?"

But he knew that if you ever have to ask for it, you're not going to get it.

"No! He must never know about you and me. It would break his heart, and he's suffered enough."

"Hey, why'd you do it in the first place? With me, I mean."

She tensed herself, threw her legs over the side of the bed, and, with some effort, sat up, patting her hair into place.

"There's one thing about you, Philip, and you must never forget it."

"What?"

"Besides your sweet and caring face, you have a very beautiful penis. It's honest, and it's full of strength. I'll leave first. Give me ten minutes. It's entirely possible this place is being watched."

He sat down on the edge of the bed and looked at the furniture. So much of it, and all so polished. So elegant, so antique. So grown up. He went to the window and after a minute or two saw her swinging jauntily up Eighth toward Montana, her bag bumping from her arm.

It was only three in the afternoon. He couldn't go home. He couldn't go back to work. He thought of going to a movie down on the Santa Monica Promenade, but what if anyone saw him?

And how could he keep quiet about whatever movie he saw? He was a really terrible liar.

Now he'd have nothing left to lie to anybody about. He was back to his regular life.

He got up, went in her bathroom to piss, then took the elevator, coming out in the bright light, blinking. No point in hiding his head now.

He drove up Eighth past Montana to San Vicente, where serious runners still ran through on the grass-green midstrip. You didn't see *them* worrying. He drove up to Twenty-sixth, turned right, saw the valet parkers still lounging at Chez Mimi. He sat in a shaded part of the courtyard, ordered a bottle of Duckhorn chardonnay, fresh tomato soup, quenelles, smoked trout, sorbet.

Did he have a broken heart? No, it felt more like relief. Was his penis really big and strong, honest—whatever she said? He would have ordered another bottle, another main course, but they'd remember him if he did, and he wanted to be able to come here again. Just to get away.

PHIL

He had been requested to attend a private meeting, URGENT, on Medical Center letterhead stationery, with CONFIDENTIAL stamped across the envelope in red. So he showed up, at Room 11345-B, in the South Wing, at ten o'clock on that Monday morning.

The room was bare except for a desk, an American flag, and a color portrait of the President—not exactly what you'd expect at UCLA—a desk and chair with a scattering of papers on it, and another chair for visitors to sit. A man in military uniform with a fair amount of ribbons got up cordially to shake Phil's hand.

"Glad you could come, Dr. Fuchs. I'm Rob Davies, Colonel

Robert Davies. Sit down, please. We've asked you here on a very important assignment for a very important reason. It wouldn't be too much to call it a mission. We'd very much like you to be a part of it. You have a real opportunity to serve the country and perhaps humanity itself."

"Sir?" Phil asked.

"A series of grants, both from the government and committed community leaders, have made it possible for us to set up a cluster of experiments and tests designed to evaluate and improve this city's response to medical emergencies. We're thinking terrorist threats, of course, but focusing especially on *medical* events. Just because bioterrorism is inefficient and carries a significant possibility of blowback doesn't mean these yahoos might not try it. We must be prepared and we *aren't* prepared. It's as simple as that."

"I'm just a dermatologist—" Phil began, but the colonel cut him off.

"Exactly! And what's a symptom of most of our historically fatal infectious diseases? The buboes of bubonic plague. The outbreak—or eruptions, whatever you call them—in smallpox. The telltale chest rash of syphilis. The whole *skin* look of typhoid, typhus. In the eventuality of a catastrophic calamitous breakout, we'd need an expert diagnosis. And fast. A dermatologist will be essential to the team. And don't worry about a security clearance. We've been looking into you. You're our man."

"I don't think I—"

"You'll be part of a group of distinguished medical experts. Six hospitals across the Los Angeles Basin and on into the Inland

Empire, as far north as Santa Barbara and south to San Diego. Six hospitals, ten men each. Needless to say, you'll be part of an elite. You'll be a leader in your own right."

"Colonel, I don't think I'm the leadership type."

"You're selling yourself short, Phil. Don't you think we know who alerted the authorities when we had that interspecies scare right on this campus? You're a man who keeps his eyes open. And you're a stable family man—relatively speaking. I think you'll know most of the people on your team." He rattled off a list of names, reading so fast from the list in his hand that Phil recognized only two of them, internist Jack Josephson, his tennis buddy, and Shackleford, the world-class asshole. And Harry Davenport, an epidemiologist so famous and *really* world-class that even Phil had heard of him, coming in for six months from Minneapolis. So Phil had said yes.

For the first Saturday-morning "mandatory training session," they'd picked the anteroom of Pediatric Dentistry, a place in the Med Center even dentists had trouble finding. No way out but two elevators, guarded by security guys. No one was getting out without making a scene, without embarrassment, without his colleagues seeing.

It was all guys in here. Where were all the bossy women, all the female Asian docs who never looked you in the eye? Where were the ones who'd kicked up such a fuss about wanting to excel and be equal and get adequate respect and jumps in promotions, because they had been so oppressed or because they were so smart? Busy at home, it looked like. Busy with other projects. Or maybe on somebody's list of suspects. Everyone in here, in folding chairs ranging along dirty-white walls, was white male, trying to maintain dignity or what looked like it. They wore their stethoscopes slung across their shoulders—well, he did too—and looked like paratroopers crouched in a plane lined up for their first jump. He sat across the room from Jack.

Three men strode in from around the corner where the dental cubicles were, Colonel Rob Davies with braid on his hat and a chest full of ribbons, a guy in that desert camouflage uniform that looked like kid's pajamas, and a measly little creep in a brown gabardine suit. He seemed like the most important one, with the worst news.

He snapped his fingers, and half a dozen burly NCOs marched in behind them, loaded up with plastic parcels stacked to their chins. The rent-a-cops had moved aside to let them pass. The man in brown snapped his fingers again, and the NCOs moved back against the wall and stood "at rest," with precision.

"We all know why we're here," the camouflage guy said. Phil didn't know who he was, didn't know why he was here, dreaded to know what was coming next.

"You will be issued, today, security suits. You are the only persons on staff to be trusted with this information and this responsibility. Today you will put on the suits, take them off, put them on, take them off, and then, observing the utmost secrecy, take them to your respective offices, where you will store them in the lower left-hand drawer of your desks."

A couple of guys were bound to object and they did object: Shackleford, the cheesy surgeon, even waved his arm and stood up.

"My desk is filled with secret files, all under lock and key. My grant information. Drafts of my work for learned journals—"

"Not anymore," the camouflage guy cut in. "As we speak, all your desks have been emptied and refitted with special storage areas. Before you leave you will be given keys, which you will wear around your necks from now on. Waking, sleeping, fucking, in the shower. Under no circumstances will you take those keys off or tell anyone—*anyone*—what those keys open."

Shackleford lifted his chin. "Is this something actually dangerous? Is this a true emergency we're looking at? Or just a training session, as we've been led to believe?"

"If the time comes to use these special suits, an alarm will sound in the Medical Center, four short blasts and one long one. This will continue for twenty minutes. When you hear this alarm, you are to leave your position—wherever you are—proceed to your office, and don your suit."

Shackleford snorted. "Some of us will be in surgery. You can't expect—"

"You will leave your position—wherever you are—proceed to your office, and don your suit."

"Our duty to the patient—"

The man in the brown suit snickered. "*Believe* me. They won't care."

Quiet in the room. Phil watched his colleagues. They seemed thoughtful. Another man spoke up. "What about the nurses, the food workers? The rest of the staff?"

"At this time, UCLA has been issued a total of thirty-seven special suits. As you know, your names have been in review for some time. You are the ones who have been chosen. Your role is to serve the common good. As other special suits are shipped to us, they will be issued to individuals on a case-by-case basis. I need not add that this material is classified at every level. You will tell no one of this, either in a family or professional context, under penalty of severe fine and federal prosecution."

"What if we're at home?" Phil heard his own voice, dry, rasping, an octave higher than it should have been.

The brown suit answered. "In that case, your duty is clear. Stay at home, promote calm in the neighborhood, reassure your families. This Medical Center and several other designated hospitals in the state will be under the strictest quarantine. No going in or out—except for the victims."

Again, Shackleford was on his feet. "You're saying—"

"The time window will have closed. Your special suit will have been confiscated and given to another physician on the list."

Davenport, the epidemiologist who was sitting next to Phil, raised his hand. "What is it we're supposed to be ready for, anthrax? Bubonic plague? Chemical weapons? Dirty bombs? Actual atomic attack?"

The three men who might have answered were silent.

Instead, the camouflage guy said, "These suits are tricky. They must be donned in less than twenty minutes. To speak plainly, if the alarm stops before you've finished suiting up, it may be academic to keep going. After the exercises here today, you will not be given any more drills, because the suits themselves are fragile in the extreme. After four wearings they become obsolete. In donning the suits, you protect the neck first. Then the fingers of both hands, the hands themselves, and the upper arms. By then you will have used approximately one third of the windings. After applying the windings, you will put on the shirt and hood. Only then do you proceed with the second part of the operation. Use the next third of the windings to wrap, closely wrap, your cock, nuts, and buttocks. Leave the pants off! Proceed to your feet, wrapping each toe separately and tightly, binding your ankles up to your calves. Then put on the pants. Only after that do you put on the boots and gloves.

"You will find, at the bottom of the parcel, a tube of transparent gel. Apply this to the borders, the *seams,* if you will, but lightly in these exercises, so that you will have enough to use in the event of a real . . . event."

"What about the mask?" Davenport asked. "You forgot the mask."

"The mask is the last item you put on," the camouflage guy said, clearly pissed. "You glue it to your head, pull down the hood, and glue that too. But don't use glue in this exercise."

"How long do we wear them?"

"Until . . . the situation changes."

"What about breathing? What about air filters?"

"It's all in there, don't worry about it. The important thing is the time frame. You may assist each other here today but when the time comes, remember, you'll be alone in your office with the doors locked. Remember the sequence! And remember to keep calm. Time is of the essence. And under no circumstances may you write the sequence down."

The enlisted men moved forward, standing in front of each

doctor, gesturing slightly with their chins. *Take one,* their expressions said. How about *them*? Would they ever get special suits? Or did they just get to hear about them?

"It's best to take off your shoes and keep on your socks, until part three of the exercise. Indeed, we recommend that from now on you wear loafers to work. In the event of an alarm, slip off your shoes and proceed directly to your offices. Remember, today, you may assist each other. Now, moving from right to left, unzip your package!"

His buddy Jack already had a partner, so Phil turned to his left, to Davenport, the world-class epidemiologist he recognized from his ID tag.

"When I started out, I got into infectious diseases because I didn't think there'd be much to do," Davenport said. "In 1975. Then there was AIDS. Then Ebola. Avian flu. Now this."

"Yeah." He was looking at what he had in his hands: moleskin. Rolls and rolls of it. *Moleskin?*

"Our necks first, right?" Davenport gamely began to wrap his own neck. "Do we go over the chin or what?"

Watching Davenport, Phil started to wind, got it too tight, could feel his cheeks heating up and starting to bulge. Davenport had a neat little beard, sort of a Freud thing. Wisps of black pubic-looking hair stuck out of the fleshy moleskin.

Davenport nodded at him, urgently. Hurry up! Get a move on!

With his right hand, Philip began winding his left. This wasn't so hard; he knew how to bandage, for God's sake. But then, when his bandaged left hand began fiddling with his right, he knew it wouldn't work. Davenport reached out and skillfully took care of him. He did the same for Davenport.

Now was the time for them to take off their pants. Awkwardly, the men turned diagonally—hell, this wasn't any worse than a locker room—but it was. Some guys wore flashy bikinis, some baggy boxers. Shackleford wore nothing at all, which should have been a surprise but wasn't. He was hung pretty well. Phil thought of the many times the guy must have dropped his pants for some woman and waited for the inevitable breathy compliment, "Oh, but you're so *big*!" Because why else would you wander around all day not wearing any underwear?

Davenport was ahead of him, winding his dick, with a couple of swipes at his balls, then leaning way down. Kissing his ass goodbye.

Things speeded up. Some of the guys, chubbier than they might have been, had trouble reaching their feet, winding every toe. And they had to leave some moleskin for last, wasn't that it? What came next? Had to be the shirt. He picked it up, shook it out. Mustard yellow, brittle nylon. Detachable hood. What about the hood? Did they attach it now? Trembling, his fists struggled with Velcro. Then buttons. This wouldn't keep out a mosquito, let alone a deadly virus.

Davenport was slamming into his pants. What held them up? Velcro. Then glue. Ridiculous. And then the mask. Davenport's face, wild now, looked out at him through plastic. There had to be a breathing apparatus, some kind of filter, but he couldn't see where. He took the mask, mashed it against his face, felt with his numbed hands for the Velcro, there it was, the stuff that made the thing stick.

A bell sounded. Philip looked sadly at green plastic boots, still folded in his package.

"Men!" the camouflage guy said with as much outrage as he could muster. "Fumblefingers! Lily livers! My God! You're the people we turn to in emergencies! You're the ones we trust our lives to. You were supposed to be the best of the best; you were the crème de la crème! You were in the top percentile. You were the ones we put our hopes on."

Silence. The guy ran out of steam. He looked off to the side, thinking about it. "All right then. We aren't leaving this room until you learn to put these suits on *right*."

The doctors ripped off their masks, sweating, furious.

"Didn't you say that after four times they'd be obsolete?"

"No way you can use this stuff four times!"

"What's with the moleskin? Didn't they use something like clear plastic over in the Gulf?"

"Yeah, but they didn't ever need it."

"What are these for anyway? Germ warfare? Chemicals? Moleskin, for Christ's sake! There's no way you can use it more than once!"

"And, look at this!" A guy yanked at the Velcro around his neck.

Across the room, Shackleford quietly inched into his plastic pants.

The three men in charge dropped back a couple of feet to the far side of the room. They spoke quietly. Colonel Davies, dignified in his naval getup, nodded, nodded again, and turned back to them.

"Gentlemen, I want you to consider that these might have been *practice* special suits, that this may have been a test instead of an actual medical experimental exercise. This might have been more of an experiment to test your reflexes, your ability to take directions. This may have been only a drill."

Davenport had taken off his mask and hood. He looked at them, held them up to the fluorescent light. "Where's the filter?" he asked. "How do we breathe in these things?"

"It's taken care of," the camouflage guy said. "It's experimental. It's in there. It's timed to activate in a timely fashion."

"I don't think so," Davenport said. "There's nothing here, that I can see."

This ticked the camouflage guy off. "You're not paid to think, soldier! You're here to do what we tell you to do! The future of the country depends on *your getting the picture* the way we tell it. This is the possible end of the world we're talking about, and there's no joke to it."

"There's no filter here," Davenport said. "You want to let us in on what you're doing?"

"This is a test. And you flunked it!"

The colonel stepped forward to say something but the camouflage guy went on. There was no stopping him now. "Just one squirt in the air vents. Or someone lights up a piece of artificial wood for a backyard barbecue or squirts some shit on some charcoal, and there goes the party! Someone drops a teaspoon of something in your cafeteria steam table, and the building goes toxic within ten minutes!"

"But you must think it dissipates fairly quickly," Davenport persisted. "It must. Because there's no breathing apparatus here."

"Get it through your head, soldier. You flunked the test. You weren't even halfway there. You're dead."

Philip took a breath, or tried to. The oxygen in this room must be giving out. Then he remembered the moleskin on his neck and began, as best he could, to unwind it.

"That's enough," he said to the camouflage guy. "He's *not* a soldier. None of us are." He picked with his right hand at his left hand and began to unwrap.

PHIL

After that it was mandatory sessions three times a week. The team of ten were given guided tours of the city, herded through LA County General Hospital with its dozens of gunshot wounds, its bulletproof glass protecting the receptionists and staff offices. Now their instructions had shifted to something like: Wherever you are when the time comes, proceed to the nearest hospital immediately. Don't worry about suits and masks, we'll have them there. (Wherever *there* might happen to be.) Basically, stow the wife and kids. Save yourself and report for duty.

They were treated to the foul halls of King Drew Medical Center, where student nurse's aides played hand-clapping games as patients languished. They toured the new building of the Rand

Corporation, where every other room appeared to be a "safe" room or could be made into one in a matter of minutes. After that particular afternoon, Phil and Jack made it next door to Chez Jay, one of the oldest, darkest, most welcoming bars in the city, downed four martinis, crossed Ocean Avenue, and spent the rest of the evening at The Lobster, which had one of the sweetest of all Los Angeles views: the vast black Pacific, of course, but the fragile Santa Monica Pier stretched out before them, and the Ferris wheel, hopefully, extravagantly lit. They meant to get drunk and did. They weren't allowed to talk about what they had seen and heard, and (honorably) didn't. But what the fuck was it that they were supposed to do? And who, in the wide world, would want to destroy such modest beauty? Just a pier. A Ferris wheel. Even Rand, with its inventory of mad scientists, was crammed with house plants, hanging plants. What was it Americans had done, Phil would think blearily, except act like assholes, and weren't everyone—wait—*wasn't* everyone some kind of asshole? "What I want to know," he asked Jack, as they both labored to free their lobsters from their shells, "is how did we get into this? What is it that we did? As a country, I mean?"

But Jack, paranoid and worried about everything, just said they could do with a little more melted butter and cut his eyes toward the table next to them. So, fine. They were being watched. "Can't anyone even find a decent job around here?" Phil asked rhetorically and then figured, *Fuck it.* There was the lobster in front of him, and lights flashing out to sea. Let it alone. Eat it.

They were taken on harbor tours—up the road to Ventura, clogged with yachts, strategically important. But not as far north as San Luis Obispo, where the atomic plant made the population goners for a hundred miles in every direction, so why bother? They were treated to Marina del Rey, slick with oil, crowded as a freeway, with its smutty little Mother's Beach, which their tour leader told them was so polluted that terrorists wouldn't even have to do anything; just stand back and wait five years and kids would start to be born with three eyes. The hospital in that region used to be called Marina Mercy but, because of its level of incompetence, was now called, affectionately, Marina Murder. (Not part of the larger network.)

And to Long Beach Harbor, where Jack whispered to Phil that in his youth he'd make the ninety-minute drive to spend the day at Acres of Books, the biggest used bookstore in the whole country, while their guide pointed out Coast Guard dinghies, tiny and impotent but with machine guns mounted, as if one stupid silly machine gun could stop the Armageddon they seemed to be waiting for—and, indeed, seemed to look forward to. They were given yet another tour of the geographically appropriate hospital, Long Beach Memorial.

They visited San Pedro Harbor—the big one for LA—and were loaded on a tour boat, where they were told to "look sharp and keep your eyes open." They were the only whites on the boat and got a lot of suspicious glances. Narcs, Phil thought. I've lived a depressing-enough life without being made as a narc. He said as much to Jack, who ignored him, went up to the full bar, and ordered them both doubles of tequila. The boat chugged through something like a maritime Kmart—not one glamorous or inviting thing about this whole body of enclosed water, although dozens of Latino families and their zillion little kids had sprung ten bucks a pop for this little hour off the shore. Just to see something different, to smell the diesel-tainted salty air.

From the civilian guide, Phil learned that American shipping had changed. There were no more ships under the U.S. flag anymore because American law required a minimum of thirty-six crew members and other countries, only seventeen. Those seventeen men wandered on ships that could carry up to 8,000 containers. Containers. That meant railroad cars. Efficiency! But Phil could already hear the lecture at the nearest safe room they'd be dragged to: Security—whatever that even meant—was always at red-alert level at this place, whatever the public knew. Because each and every one of these containers could carry a couple of hundred Chinese immigrants, or dozens of dirty bombs, or the one bomb that could take the southern part of this state right off the map and make the bay a lot bigger in the process.

Phil listened to the cheery lecture of the moment—that because this harbor was so big and had three hundred cranes that could unload ships in a thirty-six-hour turnaround, sailors hardly ever got shore leave. And that in fact there had been a Russian tugboat for hire around here for six months, and the guys had never once set foot on dry land because they didn't have visas, and wasn't that something?

They were shown Terminal Island Prison right out in the middle of the bay—and all the while Mexican-American kids were running madly around above- and belowdeck holding helium balloons their parents had bought them at Ports o' Call Village tied to their wrists, and their hardworking parents consoled themselves with ridiculous-looking "double-shot margaritas for only five dollars" dyed the same cheesy pinks and greens that the three hundred cranes had been painted. Phil and Jack soaked up their tequilas straight and learned there were only two ships in the harbor right now that actually *looked* like ships, rusty, dark, and respectable; one carried steel and nothing else, one carried coal and nothing else.

"Say," Jack called out, suddenly bold. "What about those freighters that used to carry passengers? What ever happened to them?"

The bartender looked grave. "There's still one, I think, that runs out of Marina del Rey. That's no way to travel, though. Five thousand dollars and you get to go around the world, but there's no doctor. More than twelve passengers, and you have to have a doctor."

"Wait!" Phil said. "What about these big ships here? What do they do for doctors on those?"

The bartender looked impatient. He doubled as the tour guide, and something—a buoy with sea lions—was coming up fast. "That's why we don't have ships under the American flag anymore. They require a doctor. Foreign ships need only seventeen crew members and don't need a— Just ahead on your right, folks, you'll see a group of seas lions. . . ."

After an hour's drive down and an hour's drive back, the doctors were returned to UCLA. It was a Sunday afternoon. The fresh air and alcohol had taken their toll. Phil thought, I always wanted to take the kids to see sports: NBA, NFL. What if all they'd wanted was the water, the balloons, and Felicia in all her skinny

brunetteness, drinking double-shot margaritas with paper um-
brellas? What if all they wanted was fun instead of improvement?
He thought of Felicia drinking out of a foot-long glass of sugared
tequila and letting the harbor take her. He had to smile.

The meeting afterward, back at UCLA, was more of the same.
Something terrible was going to happen. That was all they needed
to know. They were told to be vigilant, that an event of some kind
was pending, and to go on home.

They felt like they couldn't go home. Not yet.

"Man, that was worse than the Rand thing," Jack muttered.

Jack was a bachelor and sometimes Phil envied him for it, but
tonight it meant going to dark lonely rooms. And Phil couldn't go
home either.

So they left their cars in the parking lot and headed down
Westwood Boulevard as usual, to the Palomino. Just for a couple
of drinks. Everybody stopped there, once in a while, for a couple of drinks. It was a perfect California spring evening, chilling
down fast, clear and bright.

The place was packed. Not the restaurant side, which was just
beginning to fill up, but the grandiose, pretentious bar. A high,
desperate clamor came off the crowd; it was as though all of them
had been invited to an awful party and stayed around longer than
they should have for the free drinks. Most of them looked anxious
or furious. Phil and Jack pushed through to the bar and ordered
double vodkas with slices of orange. Did Phil have it wrong or did
everybody else feel the same way he did about not wanting to go
home? Had there been something bad on television?

They stood beside the bar waiting for stools. It looked like it was going to be a long wait. Phil clicked open his cell phone and called Felicia. "I'll be late. No, I don't know when I'll be home."

He realized he should have called her from out on the sidewalk so it wouldn't sound so much like a party. "You want me to bring home something?" No, she didn't.

"Don't work too hard," he told her, but she'd hung up.

He ordered another.

What was there to feel bad about? Nothing, really. It wasn't as if what was going to happen—whatever they had planned—hadn't happened to everyone before about a thousand million times. Everybody died.

"Better people than us," he said to Jack. "Better men than you. Or me, God knows."

Jack shrugged.

And it might not even happen.

"I know you!"

Phil looked over at the guy who was shouting.

But the guy wasn't talking to him. He was talking to a pudgy man with fat cheeks and a pursy little mouth, who did look familiar, actually.

The pudgy man cracked the bottom of his face in a smile. The others with him looked wary.

"You did that thing. You passed that law. Isn't that you? Weren't you on television a lot? Am I right?"

"It was an act," the pudgy man said, "not a law. That would take more than me, son. Congress passes laws. Well, they passed the Act, too."

"But it's you, isn't it? It *is* you?"

The man nodded modestly. "Yes. It is."

"Well, I want to tell you something."

"Yes?" The man held to a pleasant face.

"Want to tell you something."

The man cocked his head.

"You put something shitty in that plan of yours."

Phil ordered another double from the bartender with a wave and kept on watching. Jack stayed still.

"You took away my rights. My civil *rights*!"

They were catching attention from other people, the rambunctious crowd standing three and four deep at the bar. Out of shyness, or prudence, Phil focused his eyes, for a second or two, on all the stuff—olives, onions, cherries, lime wedges—on top of the bar, at about the level of his chest, all lit attractively from above. But he couldn't keep from hearing the voices and then looking back to the man, whose face went from pasty to ruddy in the changing bar light.

The man smiled an official smile and Phil recognized him but couldn't remember his name. He was a security guy all right, the guy in charge of carrying out some Plan. Phil's stomach crunched. What was he doing here, on this side of the country? And which one was he? The Homeland Security guy? The Born Again guy? Or the new Intelligence guy? They look alike, Phil thought. They really do. And he let out a drunken simper.

One of the guy's bodyguards, whatever, ordered another scotch. Why didn't they just leave?

Phil suddenly got it. The bunch of them must be staying over at that hotel that used to be the Marquis and was now the W. So trendy it had beds all over its lobby. Nobody real could drink there. You wouldn't see Mr. Security Man or his posse stretched out on beds drinking scotch. So they couldn't go back to the hotel. Not yet. So they came here.

"You fucked us over. Fucked us *right* over! Took away our rights! *That's* no security. That's only security for *you*."

"There have to be boundaries. That's the beauty of the law." The guard was speaking up. "We have to pull together as a country. We have to put the good of the country over personal matters. Patriotism trumps the personal." He was pretty drunk.

"Yeah?" the young man said. "Well, fuck you, you sneaking criminal." He took a swing at the security guard, who, Phil saw, through rainbows of flying olives and cherries, had to be Secret Service. Because he and his partner put the man in cuffs, right away.

"You stole my civil rights," the guy said. "I'm an American in good standing! Why'd you do it, why'd you do it? There wasn't any *Arab* made you *do* it!"

Phil got out of there, drove home the long way, out by the beach, spent the better part of an hour looking at some waves. And he thought, shivering, about those moleskin suits. And poisons. And how he was supposed to be vigilant.

And what he was supposed to do about his family.

May 2007

THE WAY
YOUNG
LOVERS
DO

ANDREA and DANNY

She'd seen him before, but she didn't get it right away, didn't realize it. It was in such a different context, and she'd never seen his face all that much. She'd sat behind him in a poetry class, a hard one, and—good girl that she was—she'd had her face down in her notebook. "Donne's Elegy Nineteen: Was it a debate between the body and soul? *No,* two men having a conversation in a bookstore!" The professor's amused voice going on and on in a cultivated northeastern accent; he was enjoying himself, but the rest of them cut the pure delicious words of the metaphysical poets with the standard student anxiety of doing well.

So she concentrated, but when she raised her head to look at the professor she saw, in front of her, a neck, belonging to a guy.

A sturdy neck, clean and clean-shaven, and broad, trim shoulders, buff. The neck the color of Asians. Why had anyone ever called that skin yellow? It was indescribable, really, not brown in any way, not white or pink or tan.

It was the color of twilight. She'd look at that neck sometimes, caught between the impossible beauty of the poetry and the familiar fear of being unexpectedly called on, the imperatives to be smart but not aggressive, pretty but not flirty, there but not there. Through the quarter, staring at his neck, listening to his low, strained, concentrating voice, she got the idea that she and he (and, yes, sure, the professor), were the only ones here in love with that language, mad about finding the meaning in those locked-up words. When he spoke, which wasn't often, there would be a silence afterward in the class, a deference on the part of everybody, because he knew what he was talking about. And while he was speaking she'd rest her gaze on his neck, his shoulders, his perfectly pressed shirt. His shoulder muscles tensed when he spoke.

It was only an undergraduate poetry class. After ten weeks she got her A and moved on. There was enough to think about at home. Her mother, pinched and plainly terrified, worried sick about her dad, making several cakes at a time, or a set of apple pies, or playing Strauss waltzes at four in the afternoon on their big square piano, or puttering in their terraced garden past the French windows along the back of the house. Because if she was cooking or grading papers or playing the piano and everything in sight was spotless and fresh and cared for, what could possibly be wrong? Or she spent time down in the waiting room of the Med

Center, to be near to her husband, whiling away time, keeping awful things at bay.

But then at four thirty—and Andrea would already be home; the walk from campus was short and she didn't mind living at home, wanted to, needed to—the door to the study would open and her father would emerge, tranced and spaced out from six or eight hours of translating, sitting at a special desk, one of only two like that in Southern California, a chair and a desk all in one piece made of bentwood, made so you could sit and work without pain for hours at a time. But now he spent three mornings a week down at the Medical Center while they filtered his blood. Now his days were very full, teaching at the university and translating that Serbian novel and watching bad television down at the dialysis place. They couldn't clean his blood enough, that was the problem.

She could see, looking at her father, the pale greens and blues that showed up under his eyes in the late afternoon, the stiffness of his fatigue, the whole soreness of his illness, the great generosity of his spirit as he strove to overcome these things and take the philosophical position that everything was fine. He complimented the cakes, poured himself a glass of wine, allowed a shy hand to rest on his daughter's shoulders or hair, wandered, whistling, through the house, rotating his shoulders to get out the kinks, and the terror would settle in their living room. Her mother would sigh. Andrea remembered that poem—was it George Herbert or Herbert of Cherbury?—about death being with us from the time we're born, our swaddling clothes are really our winding sheets, and let's not fool ourselves about it.

Then they'd have dinner, not so many people over anymore, and her dad would talk about problems in the translation he was working on or what was going on in the department, since he and her mom both worked there, sharing one full-time position. And Andrea would want to scream or cry. She'd talk about her classes. The silence, the isolation, the sadness would shut down on all of them. At ten her dad would remark ritualistically, "Well, it's a school night," and walk quietly into the master bedroom. Almost every night in his life, she thought, had been a school night. He wanted to live with the blaze of language inside his head, a dozen elegant eastern European languages. He loved to teach, and she knew it; she'd taken his classes; he was wonderful. Her mother was very good too. She worked hard.

Andrea's dad was dying. She was nineteen and a sophomore at UCLA. She lived at home and her father was dying. He would actually die.

Pretty often she went with her mom and dad down to the UCLA Med Center, where the feeling was that he was getting a little worse.

She'd sit in the waiting room with her mother, who'd often pull up a chair and talk to the lady at the reception desk. She'd apply herself to her homework, and sometimes she'd look at her own forearm's golden tan, or watch the veil of hair that hung down as she hunched over her books, that requisite golden blond. She knew she was beautiful but she wasn't sure what good it was supposed to do. Plenty of dates with large rough boys in high school, a certain amount of envy from her girlfriends, and now, at UCLA, a ring of hostility or deference that persisted around her wherever she went. Which might be what she and that Asian guy shared, a place at the center of a circle of deference, an isolation that could make you weep.

In the waiting room at the Med Center, she'd watched the Chinese family and the rest of their relatives this past week with a touch of irritated contempt; they had an uncle on a respirator and couldn't bring themselves to pull the plug, but they certainly weren't the only ones in this place suffering. What a lot of noise they made! She focused on the women and felt her mother's own stiff disapproval beside her. The men were just a tapestry of exotic tattooed guys, until she asked her mother if she could bring her anything and went down the hall and into the cafeteria for apple juice and coffee and saw him, his neck, his back to her, picking up some mineral water. He felt her gaze immediately; his muscles tightened. She spied the ink-blue tail of something, half an inch of it, snaking up his neck from his shirt collar. He turned around and she lowered her eyes, blushing.

"You were in Post's class," he said.

She nodded.

"What's your name again?"

She was perfectly sure he knew her name. "Andrea Barclay."

"What kind of name is that?" His lame idea of a joke.

"English."

"Lee. Chinese."

She nodded again.

They'd paid for their drinks by now.

"Want to sit down?"

"My mother. . . ."

He wouldn't meet her eyes, looked off, indifferent-seeming, waiting. But she had the advantage; she'd seen his muscles tense as he answered questions before.

"For a little while," she said. "I guess I can."

They sat down at a Formica table in the middle of the big room. Nothing to say to each other. She looked at him, and his eyes, focusing on air four feet away from her, moved back and met her own.

"I knew you," he said. "I knew you when I saw you."

"I know."

He shrugged, and a shiver went through his body. He sighed heavily, almost a groan, and reached out and took her hand.

He pulled her to her feet, took her down a long side hall, avoiding the waiting room, and pushed out the side door, walked her up a little hill, a road on this bright campus, where across the street another building was being thrown up—more cream-colored bricks and travertine. He turned a sharp right off into what they still called the Botanical Garden. Eucalyptus. Acacia. Sumac, inches of dry sharp leaves under their feet. And shade. It was hot outside the boundaries, but in here it was hot gray blue.

He pulled her down to the side of another building, window-less, stood with his back to it, looking at her. She was the one who put her hands on each side of his beautiful, helpless face and kissed him, had to kiss him first. But he wasn't a boy. His arms were hard as iron, not very gentle. She gasped and he let her go.

"I have to show you something," he said, breathing hard.

Before she could laugh or draw away or be frightened, or think how silly the words sounded, he turned his back to her, and unbuttoned his shirt. His beautiful back. Covered with tattooists' handiwork.

"That's my life, my whole life there. You should see it first. And you should think, Andrea! You should really think. I'm not the same as you."

But she could only kiss the back of his neck, where the tail of a mythic dragon started. His whole body shuddered. He turned around and held her in his arms, breathing deeply. Later she would try to figure it out, how it had happened, where he got his incredible strength—well, he weight-lifted, of course. His body was nothing but muscle, just a little bit reptilian, as if he were a python or an anaconda. He wasn't just *in* his body, thinking about what he was doing or what he might be doing next or what kind of moves he might best make. He *was* his body.

He was not tall. He was maybe two inches taller than she but then they were standing on a steep embankment, he leaning back against that stucco wall, she just a little above him. He held her, not moving, and remembering it later that night, safe in her room, in her comfortable, immaculate clean sheets, she could only remember that first hour in shards, clippings. He smelled of eucalyptus, and thin threads of sunlight sifted across his intent face. She didn't think of him making love to her, it was she who couldn't get enough of him, stroking the sides of his face, kissing his neck again and again, breathing him in as deeply as she could. Way too well brought up to even think of taking off her clothes in public, on campus, in the daytime, she could only press up against him, flattening her breasts against his chest, locking her arms around his neck, feeling his—what did you even call *it*? She had been out with dickheads, certainly, often, and they were more than fond of whipping out their dicks, trying to get her to do something or other, and sometimes she did and sometimes she didn't, but afterward, always, she and her girlfriends laughed about it on the phone.

Now, later, she didn't know what to call it. There were no words for it. The python part of him, but he was all part python, really. With a story on his back, waiting for her to decipher. Back home that night, sore, wrung out, chapped on every part of her body, she thought about her father. He spent his life deciphering things, trying to get at the meanings of things. Decoding, she thought. Decoding Danny.

Locked and silent, motionless, she was the one who first said *please,* and she felt a shift in his weight, the muscles in his thighs moved against hers, and, still standing, she could only say *please* again.

He took her hand and they lay down in a bed of dry leaves. They were so sheltered that leaves brushed against his hair.

Then they did it, mediumly or slow, she couldn't remember, but when he was done he stayed lying on top of her, and when he did remember to say, "Am I hurting you? Lying on you like this?" the way guys sometimes did, and they were really saying, How can I not be hurting you? I am so strong and mighty! Part of their overall performance, and you were supposed to say, Oh, no! or Yes, just a little—whatever might please them most, he was just coming to, up out of the most profound trance, and really seemed to be concerned that he might be hurting her, might have hurt her.

It was still before noon. She looked at his face, close up. It might be called a hard face. So she looked further, more closely, at his beautiful twilit skin.

"We have to go back," he said. "We have to go back inside."

"Yes."

"You go first."

"Yes."

He handed her her panties and the rest, which she put on, searched for her shoes. He found them for her.

She scrambled up the embankment, blinked in the sun, went in the side door they'd come out of, went to a ladies' room, cleaned herself up, using paper towels and liquid soap. Combed her hair. Her cheeks were burning. She looked stoned to herself, on drugs. She went to the cafeteria, got three Diet Cokes, drank one off right away, and took the other two back to the waiting room.

He was already there, back against the wall, impassive, watching and not watching his mother and sisters. The doctor came out and spoke to them, and the mother wept bitterly. Shook her head.

After an hour or so he left and came back after another hour. Then glanced at her as he got up to leave again.

"Is it OK with you, Mom, if I go home a little early? I need to get something at the library."

"Yes . . . dear." She looked concerned.

"It might take me awhile," Andrea said. "I'm looking for some things. Don't worry if I'm a little late."

"Just be home for dinner?"

"Sure."

After her daughter left, Melinda got up and went to sit by Edith, who, for lack of a better word, had become her friend by now.

"Am I imagining things?" she asked. "Tell me I'm imagining things."

Edith hesitated, her sharp, intelligent face holding itself in abeyance, thinking over what to say. "I don't think so," she said.

Melinda shook her head. "Jesus, Mary, and Joseph! At a time like this. And right in front of me."

"It's the death all around," Edith said plainly. "God knows, I've done it myself. And a lot of other people have too."

Melinda shook her head again and laughed. "She could at least have brushed some of the twigs off her sweater!"

"Give her a break, if you can," Edith said. "She's a sweet girl. Can you cut her some slack? And yourself too?"

It was around three in the afternoon when Andrea took the side door out of the place, walked the eighth of a block up a street, and noticed that the construction workers had gone home. She balanced on the edge of the sidewalk, thinking for the first time that she might have been mistaken, misread his signal, when she heard his voice, both soft and hard: "Over here."

She turned a little to her left and ducked into the underbrush, into a different world. He'd made a little clearing, a cave, with a blanket on the ground, two pillows. Two bottles of drinking water. He lay down on the ground, propped up on an elbow. She could see easily enough now; he was plainly terrified. And she, so self-conscious she could barely move.

But she did.

She was a little late for dinner. Her mother said, "Are you all right?" And her dad said she looked a little feverish.

"I'm tired, is all. Is it OK if I just skip dinner and get a snack later?"

Could they have known? How could they *not* have known?

She took off her clothes and looked in the mirror as she ran a bath. She thought of his back. Her body told a story too. There were bruises and scratches all over her arms and legs. Her breasts swollen and bluish. As she looked at them, took note of them, they started to throb all over again. She remembered, bemused and amazed, especially when she compared this with what she'd done with other men—boys, actually—and their anxious, demanding questions. Did you come yet? Did you come? Are you coming? He hadn't ever asked. He was strong, and strung her along, and she jolted her way through the afternoon, thinking of nothing and nobody else.

They said as little as they could and lay exhausted, until, somewhere around six, the sun on its way down, he barely whispered, close to her ear, " 'I wonder by my troth . . .' "

And she answered, in another world, " 'What thou and I didst . . .' "

And heard him, wondering, " 'Till we loved.' "

The next morning her mother was up early, squeezing orange juice. "I want you to know, Andrea . . ."

She waited, apprehensive.

"How much your dad and I love you. You mean the world to us. You know that, don't you?"

So she went to class, drenched in love.

DANNY and ANDREA

Her house was an easy walk from campus. She wanted them to walk and there was no reason not to, but he felt naked without his car. Did he imagine it? Were the students who shambled in the other direction from the dorms and the fraternities in flip-flops, burdened down with backpacks, looking at them? Looking at the beautiful blonde, the tough Chinese? In another place, another time, he would have collared one of them, some big Caucasian guy, and said, with all the menace in the world, "Hey! You looking at *me*?" And cliché or not, the guy would say *No, no*! fifty times, because beyond the cliché there would be the real threat of harm.

Three in the afternoon, on the well-traveled path from campus to the dorms, and soft sunlight was checkered by dozens of eucalyptus and jacaranda trees. Beyond the dorms, on one of the residential streets going up the hill, she quickened her pace, heading for home. On the east side of LA where he lived, women still usually walked behind men, whining or whispering, but there she was out in front. Three days since they'd met—talked—in the cafeteria.

"Wait up," he said. "I don't want to show up there in a lather like a goddamned racehorse." He was so far away from any land he knew.

She turned, reached up, put her hand on his head, skimming his hair. "It's just coffee. And you've seen them before."

He tried for a menacing grunt but it didn't work.

"Come on," she said. "It won't be so bad. They're nice. Honestly."

A cool breeze chilled him. He was sweating.

Hedged sloping lawns, thick vines full of pink roses, arches with more roses, sprinklers sweeping lazily, a smell of flowers: fucking Arcadia. Nobody around, though. Kind of a tomb feeling about it. If these people didn't ever get in any trouble, what did they do? How did they spend their time?

She turned to the right, went up some redwood steps set in a damp green lawn. At the door she reached for her key, but the door opened and there was her mom.

"Oh! I hoped it was you! It *is* Danny, isn't it? Andrea told me we'd seen each other in the waiting room but I couldn't quite recall!" She was blushing. "I'm afraid I thought that story might be apocryphal!"

For about a hundred years his mind searched for something to say and then gave up.

"Mom," Andrea said, but her mother went on.

"Come in, come in, what a lovely surprise. Didn't you and Andrea have a class together? Excuse the house, it's in disarray, I'm afraid, since my husband hasn't been himself, I haven't had time. . . . Come in, come in. . . . It is Danny, isn't it? How nice that you stopped by."

He kept his eyes down, furtively surveying the territory, which looked like a movie set to him, or a place in a novel, certainly a place he'd never been in his life. To his left, just inside the door, a big shining square piano. To his right, a couple of sofas, pretty old. Books floor to ceiling. Music stuff on the piano. And a big round table farther on, over in the big room, with old chairs. Dust in the air, he couldn't help noticing.

"Sit down over here . . . Danny. Would you like tea or coffee? I have sherry too. I've made cookies, just to keep myself busy. What's your major? I so rarely get over to the actual campus anymore except to teach my classes, but it's beautiful, don't you think? The botanists, the gardeners, are the actual heroes over there, far more than the professors. . . . I *love* what they're doing!"

"Coffee, please."

His voice carried so much threat that even Andrea looked dismayed.

The mother shrank back. She was frail and drawn, a world away from her fresh, peachy daughter. "Sit down, please. I'll be right back."

Well, what am I supposed to do about it? He put his hands in his lap and then defiantly flat on the table. What if he broke one of these rickety chairs? Not from weight but from energy? What if he pounded the piano with his fists until it broke?

Then a tray of cookies appeared, and three little cups in three little saucers and little white napkins, and the mom sat down with them and arched her brows. He was expected to talk, but what in the world was he supposed to say? He never even talked to his own mother except to tell her to quiet down.

I can't, he said silently to the blond girl, to Andrea. *I don't know how to do this.*

"So, Danny! Did I ask you? What's your major? How long have you been going to UCLA?"

The poor woman was about to faint.

"I'm an English major. I do go to school here. But my uncle was in an accident. A car accident. That's why I'm here. Was there. In the Medical Center. My mom is real upset."

"How awful for you!"

A door opened and there was Andrea's father. Danny knew enough to stand. The dad looked bleary. He eyed the others in the room and smiled. "I've seen you before," he said.

"Yes."

Why couldn't he just *talk*? Because English was his second language? No. Because he couldn't. He couldn't.

"Too much Hungarian gives me a headache. After an hour or two, I'm through."

"Oh, Daddy."

What was this place of fond smiles and jittery fear? Because if there was one thing he could do, it was pick up on fear, and this place was thick with it.

"Danny's an English major, Daddy. But he speaks fluent Cantonese."

"I envy you. My only languages are Western." The man was mild and sad. I can't take this, Danny thought. *Sad* is out of the picture.

"Doesn't do me much good. Cantonese."

Andrea's dad nodded. "Sometimes I wonder about translation. How any of us can presume to understand anything, even in our own language. But it's too late now."

"Listen," Andrea said, "we've got to be going. We've both got exams tomorrow. We just thought we'd stop by. I'll be home later on tonight." She spoke as she moved, carrying cups out to the kitchen. "Come on, Dan. We don't want to be late."

"It was so nice to meet you," her mother said. "I'm sure we'll see each other again. Don't study too hard now! I hope your uncle feels better soon."

He didn't say anything, just nodded his head and allowed himself to be led out into the sun by the girl. But out on the sidewalk this time he took the lead and she was the one to say, "Hey! Wait up!"

He kept his head set three quarters away from where she was, and she had to skip along, to bob in front of him to say, "What is it?" and then say it again.

"What is it?"

After half a block he muttered, "I can't do this."

"Do what?"

They walked along, back the way they came.

He was walking in front of her to Parking Lot Four. He thought of his car as a refuge now, the leather seats, wood dash-board, loud gears, rough CDs. He would drive with the window down, smoking, sleeves rolled to show some of his tattoos, music shrieking. But where would he go?

Not home.

Not back to the dorms.

Not back down to the waiting room, certainly.

He walked rapidly, trying to get shut of her. But as they got to the lot she took hold of his arm like some trembling grandma and they turned to go in another direction, southwest through cam-pus. He knew where she was going and took shallow breaths. They went back down into the Botanical Gardens. It was later now, six o'clock, an early fog coming in. She held his arm with both her hands and they walked until they found their place. His arms, his legs, his dick did the work for him, and she locked him in, in this green world where words of any kind didn't count for shit.

DANNY and ANDREA

"You know, once when I was down in Chinatown? The real one, not the tourist one? A couple of Caucasian ladies came into this restaurant, a real Chinese one, and she ordered off the Chinese menu. The waiter said, 'Something's in there you not gonna like.' Right about that time they unloaded a carton of live eels from a truck outside and the carton broke, or fell, whatever. Jeez, you should have seen the guys trying to pick them up. It was hot that day—"

"Was there?" Andrea asked.

"Was there what?"

"Something in the soup?"

"I don't know. You sure you want to do this?"

"Whatever you want."

"Things are different now, I guess. More cosmopolitan. I mean, the Empress Pavilion. Bankers from Hong Kong. But not with us. Don't expect much."

"Much what?" They were stuck in traffic, eastbound, just out of downtown, coming up on Cal State LA and the County Hospital, gridlocked on the way to Monterey Park.

"Decoration."

"Danny?"

He raised his shoulders, kept his hands on the wheel. "I'm just saying. Don't expect much."

She didn't say anything.

"There'll only be about half of them there. There's always somebody back with Uncle Lao."

"Danny, I must have seen them all a dozen times. Twenty times, even. Won't they know who I am?"

He shrugged. He wasn't going to say that because she was Caucasian they wouldn't have noticed her, and because she was a woman they *really* wouldn't have seen her.

"I didn't tell them about you yet.

"Because," he continued into her silence, "for one thing, it's none of their business. But you ought to know them. You know what I mean."

She drew in a breath.

"I mean, you showed me to your mom. Right away. Tough Chinatown boy."

"What does *that* mean?"

"I don't know what I can give you," he said. "I don't know why you're with me, even for a week."

"Fishing for compliments?" She put her hand on his thigh.

"Man, I don't know. You're driving me nuts." Couldn't he maybe just say that he didn't have the language for this, that his chest felt like jelly with her around, that he felt admiration for her innocence and jealousy of her goodness, that she was like honey to him but that he didn't know how to act, didn't have the beginning of a clue? That he really was like all those things people talked about, a turtle without a shell, a soldier without a shield; that he was defenseless around her, he, a guy whose defenses had been perfect, more than perfect, for so long?

"It's just me, you know," she said. She looked at him with so much affection that he thought his head might explode.

"We don't do that in our culture."

"What?"

"What you do."

"What's that? What do you mean?"

What was he going to say? That no one had ever looked at him with love? That the most he had gotten from anybody so far in his life was respect at the best and fear at the worst?

"Are you for real?" Tough-talking. Again.

"I don't know."

They glided down the off-ramp. The signs out here, most of them, were in Chinese by now. The people on the sidewalks were Asian.

"It's just an apartment. They live in an apartment. They've

only been here about twenty years. That's not very long. There're still a few cousins left in the home village. They don't want to come over. My mom and her brothers and sisters, they don't want to go back. Life was hard over there. One war after another." He'd never been a talker. Now listen to him. "That's it," he said. "Right here."

The three-story building stretched half a block. White concrete, and then sidewalk, and then the street. Little balconies jutted out, cluttered with bicycles or geraniums; off one railing, a Chinese peasant jacket hung out to dry in the old way, strung along a stick of bamboo. He clicked the remote control, and the parking lot door slid open.

"We won't stay long."

"Whatever you want."

His sister Lan opened the door.

"Andrea, this is my sister Lan." He moved Andrea on through: the first Caucasian, to his knowledge, who had ever been in the place. "This is it," he said, and by that he meant the dark brown shag rug, the high horizontal windows close to the ceiling, the two uncles at the Formica table playing *fan,* another sister who came out of the kitchen and just looked, the beat-up furniture, the smell of soy and sesame and ginger and onions and cooking oil smoked up way too hot; the heat of the place itself, up near ninety degrees, those two uncles, scrawny and astonished.

"This is my older sister, May. Andrea, May."

May spoke to him in Chinese. *"Ma is going to kill you dead. Why didn't you tell us you were coming?"*

"Hi," Andrea said. "I'm glad to meet you."

May turned around and went back into the kitchen.

"Sit down," he told Andrea. "There on the couch. Watch some TV. I'll get us a Coke."

"You're going to catch it," May told him in Cantonese. *"I don't want to be here when you catch it."*

"We just stopped by for a minute. I need to pick up some CDs."

"You think we're on exhibit for your pleasure? You think we're a joke for you to laugh at? Think again, Danny!"

"Please. Keep it down." He pushed past her, rummaged in the refrigerator. No Coke, of course. Just leftover Chinese food, some of it spoiling. Well. His ma didn't have much time right now.

May was warming up. *"Bring her in here in the kitchen, why don't you! Bring her in to look at our things! Shameful, conceited kick-ass!"* All this in Cantonese.

He balled his fist at her. "Shut up!"

"Or what, conceited? You'd hit your sister?"

May. His sister. His older sister by five years, and late coming to this country. Shorter than he by an inch or two, far from a beauty, with a flat face, flecked with an unattractive sweat that made her cheeks shine. She was out of China, but she was done for. She'd marry a man who looked and thought like their uncles and have some kids who'd treat her with contempt. But what about me? he thought. Can't I have something different? Something better?

"Can't you even get a Coke in this house?" He heard his own voice, the voice of a child talking, *Siao di di.* He was just her little brother, after all.

"You better pray Ma doesn't come home when she's here!"

"You don't know anything," he said. "You just think you do," and left the kitchen.

Andrea and Lan were sitting side by side on the couch, watching *General Hospital.*

"Hey," he said. "Maybe we'd better go."

"No, stay," Lan offered unexpectedly. "We're watching TV." This, in English.

"You OK?" he muttered.

"I'm fine." But of course she'd heard the words from the kitchen.

"Danny. You got a girlfriend? Introduce us." It was Uncle Ming. He'd never find a girl himself. Never get out of his sister's apartment.

Danny ignored his uncle. "Come on, let's go."

Andrea got to her feet and nodded to Lan. "It was nice to meet you." And nodded, a bare tentative tilt of the head, to the men in the corner.

But May came out of the kitchen. She wasn't through.

"He bring you on over, then he take you on *out!*" she said, in accented English. "Maybe he think you're too good for us? I tell him, Wait until our ma come home, so she can get a look at you!"

"Shut up, May!"

"I'd like to meet your mom," Andrea began, but he took her arm.

"We're going now."

As they pulled the door shut and went downstairs, voices followed them: excited, angry, insulted.

"What are they saying?"

"Nothing. They don't know anything."

As they walked to the car he saw that she too was sweating, clear non-oily drops forming at her hairline, sliding down her temple.

"They've had a hard time in this country," he said. "They got out of one bad thing, but they couldn't know what they were getting into. I think they're *lost*, you know? Homesick, but they can't go home. They don't mean anything. What they say."

"We should drive a little," she said, once they were in the car. "We could go out to the beach."

He drove the Santa Monica Freeway and then the 405 up to Sunset, west. Into the land of the white man. Desolate to him.

"Let's go farther."

He drove farther west, almost to the beach, and turned right to Los Liones, the trailhead to Topanga Canyon, where they ditched the car, hiked maybe a mile in, turned off the trail into a patch of green, lay down in the warm shade. Holding on for dear life.

"This isn't what I thought it would be," she said.

"I know. I know."

BE THOU
MY VISION

PHIL

"You know what my stepfather said? He can get us into the Tennis Club."

"What?"

"The Beverly Hills Tennis Club. In fact, he already put up our names. I told him I'd talk to you about it."

"But we already have the Rec Center." It was one of his favorite places, calm and on the campus, filled with decent professional people.

"We deserve better. *You* deserve better."

Phil hadn't the heart to tell her, but the Tennis Club wasn't all that better.

"Can we talk about it later?"

"He said he'd put up the entrance fee. That was nice of him, Phil."

"Why are you doing this now? Why didn't you ask me first?"

"Well"—she pulled up a kitchen chair to the counter, patted it, motioned for him to sit down—"two reasons. You know, Eloise is going to turn sixteen."

"So?" He'd thought a car, the Audi that doctors' daughters loved, would be pretty much the whole story. That and a family dinner. That and a party for her friends. Maybe a trip to Tahoe.

"So, in two years, she'll be eighteen." She waited for him to get it, then sighed. "That's a big birthday. And high school graduation. Then college. Then she'll be getting married! You can't do those things at the Rec Center!"

"I don't get it."

"Phil. Please. Anyway, there's another reason. Another whole reason. You don't remember, do you?" Again, she looked at him, waited, then gave it up. "I'll be turning forty. In just a few weeks."

He patted her hand. "We all have to go sometime."

She didn't laugh. "Al said a party at the club might be nice. And increase our chances for membership. Something really nice, not grand really, but something nice. And *don't* say you were going to do something yourself, because you *never* do something! You didn't even remember when it was until I reminded you! Besides, he wants us to be members."

"What's with this Al, all of a sudden? I thought you couldn't stand the guy!"

"He's all right. This was his idea." The way she said it made him know it was her idea. "I'm going to be forty. Half my life over—"

"If you're lucky!" he interrupted, but she didn't appreciate his jokes.

"It's just like you to say that. What *I* want to know is why you want to deny me this simple request too?"

"What's the *too*?"

"You know what I mean."

"No, I don't."

"You deny me another baby, and the avocado farm. You won't let us move to another state. You won't deal with Vern!"

"*Je*sus, Felicia!"

"You can say all you want, but you know it's true. If there's anything I ever want in the world, you do everything you can to keep me from getting it. You only think about yourself, you know that? You can't see one inch beyond your own face."

"Wait! Wait a minute! *I'm* the one who's been trying to get you to focus on the world! You hole up here in the house and worry about I don't know what-all—"

"I suppose you want me to go to law school," she said bitterly. "Spend my old age in law school. But I've told you before I'm not that kind of woman! I'm a woman who's chosen to stay home with my children!"

A lot of good it's done, he thought. But he didn't say it. He knew she wasn't that bright, thought secretly she might be the reason Vernon was turning into what he was, ever since he'd happened upon one of her handwritten recipes for chocolate cheap cookies, instead of chip. He couldn't see how to get into her mind.

"I don't understand you," he said, and she said, full of sad triumph, "No. You don't."

"Whatever," he said. "Do what you want."

"But you'll keep up the membership? He'll do the entrance fee and you do the annual fees?"

"Sure. Sure. Do you want us to give up the Rec Center?"

"Certainly not! Where would you play tennis?"

At the tennis club? he wanted to answer, but he didn't.

The next Sunday they went to lunch at the club with Janet, Felicia's mom, and Al, the stepdad. The kids came too, but they headed straight for the pool. From where he sat, Phil could see them: Eloise, languid, on her back, nursing her tan (no matter what he told her!); Vernon, standing on the short board, belly flopping, surfacing, blowing his nose in his hand, climbing out, trotting half the length of the pool, belly flopping again, driving seniors out and little kids down to the shallow end.

He could see all this because the club wasn't that big. It was nice—five or six tennis courts and the decent pool and a nice enough dining room—but he would have picked the Rec Center anytime, with its brown wood, its vast pool, its many rooms for readings and lectures. He and Felicia had always had different ideas about the good life.

The people here were slim and tan. They wore cream-colored slacks and cream-colored shoes. They reminded him of his in-laws. Well, they *were* his in-laws, come to think of it, and the people they hung with.

Felicia looked pretty, but she was tense. She had a thing she did when she was tense; she put her right hand up along her left collarbone as though she were having a heart attack. Or keeping her chest from falling off. There was another couple at the table, about their age. He was sitting next to the woman.

"So," Phil said. "What's your name again?"

"Barbara," she said.

"And you're with . . ."

"Larry."

Across the table, Larry was holding forth to Felicia's mother. Larry had walked in showing a fair amount of tanned calf and thigh under his nicely creased shorts. He wore a teal blue polo shirt. He looked good and he knew it.

"The situation is far more difficult than the media are telling us," he told Felicia's mom, after nodding curtly in Phil's direction. "We know there's a shadow government in place, ready to take over if need be. We know about the bunkers under every George-town home that matters. We know the government knew about the attacks and allowed them to happen—"

"It's just about oil, isn't it? Everybody wanting it? And money?" Phil threw out—and endured the appraising glances of the five other adults.

"I'm afraid it's a good deal more complex than that," Larry answered gravely.

Phil ordered a Bloody Mary.

"This situation has been in the works since the teens of the last century. When the Ottoman Empire fell it was Winston Churchill—or maybe his father—who engineered a deal, putting together a series of Middle Eastern nations divided according to their *insecurities*. The thought was to make the countries weak by keeping tribal animosities strong."

A waiter came over. Did they want to order from the buffet or from the menu?

"When Churchill got out, he really didn't get *out*. He wrote—and made sure it would be found in his correspondence—that he was tired of protecting an ungrateful citizenry. He was being ironic, as everyone knew. He left the footprints of the British Lion all over the region."

"I'll take the buffet, I guess," Phil said. "What about the rest of you?"

"I don't know," Felicia said. "What about you, Mother?"

"I'll have the salad. That crab and avocado. They do it so well."

"That's what I'll have too."

Beside him, Phil felt Barbara tense up to speak, but no one asked her.

Phil got up and went to the buffet. He couldn't help it, he went straight for the waffles.

They took a while to make, and when he came back Larry was still running his mouth.

". . . Communism was the *true* red herring. From that point of view Truman was right. A fifty-year waste of time or, more likely, a clever shell game. Of course, Britain miscalculated fifty years before *that*, when they lost the Opium War and opened the door to yet another series of conflicts, *drug* wars."

"Wait," Phil said. "They won the Opium War. I remember

that from college. England made China buy the opium. England got rich so China lost the war."

"England lost the war, but her ambitions were global, still are. If you look at the names of the companies imprinted on the pipes of the oil companies all across the Middle East, you'll find that the names are British, not American."

"Amazing," Felicia said. "So interesting."

"The British Lion watched as America depleted its resources in a wasteful conflict with the 'red menace,' a phantom menace as it turned out."

"What does Larry do?" Phil asked the woman next to him— Barbara.

"He's in security," she said.

"What kind of security?"

"I don't know."

"How long have you known him?"

"Just since this morning. After tennis, he invited me to breakfast."

"The world situation is far more dangerous now than at any other time in the history of our nation, perhaps of the civilized world."

Phil was on his third Bloody Mary by now. Time slowed, then stopped. He watched Vernon, moving like a graphic on a computer, the only thing that made sense in his field of vision.

"Yeah?" Phil said thickly. "Suppose you're right? What are we supposed to do about it? Except for staying out of New York." Low-grade. These people were so low-grade.

Larry turned in his chair. It was strange, how even if you

weren't drinking very much, but nobody else was drinking, it looked like you were the one who was really drinking.

"We can keep our eyes open. Use our common sense. Protect those around us." He glanced at Felicia. "We can prepare. We can elect to live in a state of vigilant preparedness."

The next afternoon when Phil came home he found the kitchen counters stacked with Campbell's soups and Dinty Moore beef stew.

"I can't believe it! You really paid attention to that guy? You've already done this twice, and then we had to give it all to some food bank!"

"Everyone's doing it. Look. I got scotch in plastic bottles. That way it won't break during an explosion."

"We don't drink scotch, honey!"

"I know that. That's my reasoning. If we don't like it, we won't be tempted to *drink* it. That way it will be there when we need it. And I got instant coffee. And I've been to the drugstore. They're putting together Care packages. I put our name down. They're waiting for rubber gloves."

"Felicia. What if nothing happens?"

"Yes, but what if it does? How would I feel if I hadn't done anything?"

"You know that thing about the Opium War? He was wrong about that. The Chinese lost that war. They really did."

"Oh, Phil, can't you see? It doesn't even matter!"

The door opened and Eloise came in.

"Hi, hon," her dad said.

She didn't answer him, gave her mother a standard look of scorn. Or was it something else? Tossed her hair, sneered at the cans on the sink, and disappeared into the hall and presumably up to her room.

"I have the application," Felicia said. "To the Tennis Club."

"You sure you want to do this?"

"Yes."

"What about Vern? Are you going to take him to a doctor or what?"

"He hates me! I don't know why! He's disrespectful, he has no manners, he won't bathe! I think he's going to kill me one day, I really do. And *you* certainly won't do anything about it."

She hadn't answered him, of course. And to be truthful, he didn't have a fucking clue about what to do with the kid. If anything.

"All right," he said. He just wasn't up for another round of this. "Where do you want the cans, in the kitchen cupboards? Do you think you have room?"

"No. The inside closet by the powder room. We can seal it with tape if we have to. Did you . . . what did you think of Larry?"

"Larry? He's an asshole."

"Some people would say he's a very interesting man."

"The Chinese didn't win the Opium War, Felicia!" He went into the bar under the stairs and opened some decent wine.

PHIL

FROM: Philip Fuchs, MD
TO: Colonel Robert Davies
CONFIDENTIAL: FOR YOUR EYES ONLY

The initial patient presented with a rasping cough, fever of 102°, inflamed throat and eardrums, acute sore throat, swollen glands, a fiery rash, swollen extremities. She was accompanied by her mother and sister. The three were immediately issued surgical masks, as were the nurses and other patients who had been seated within a twenty-foot radius in the waiting room. The volunteer at the information desk was issued a mask as well.

The patient complained of severe abdominal pain and displayed increasing agitation. She complained of the sound of tennis balls in a tournament being shown on television, but at that time the television set was turned off.

By this time she was in isolation, but because of their previous mutual exposure, her mother and sister were allowed to remain with her. Social workers and medical assistants were dispatched to their home, where two other children remained. Another was sent to the patient's husband's place of work. He returned home. The family has been put under quarantine.

The patient did not fit the SARS profile or any other known profile. The exception—the significant symptomatic exception—continued to be her grossly swollen extremities. By the second day of hospitalization her fingers and toes had split at the tips. The tissue rapidly became necrotic.

This is not, however, what is popularly referred to as an example of "flesh-eating bacteria." The necrosis remained rooted in the extremities. The patient was administered Cipro and Demerol for pain. She remained in good spirits. Approximately 12 hours after the patient's admission, her sister exhibited the same sore throat, high fever, and splitting of the extremities. (The three, at their request, were allowed to remain together.)

The patients' vital signs remained more or less stable during the first two days. All staff maintained the highest possible security precautions, both in medical and media terms. An explanation was put forth that two "high-class wives" from the United Arab Emirates had come down with chicken pox, but that since their religious beliefs required the strict observation of purdah, only minimal staff was allowed in, a total of four nurses around the clock and two physicians, Dr. Philip Fuchs and Dr. Harold Davenport.

All six involved staffers observed hospital quarantine, remaining indoors in the C-A section on the fifth floor of the facility. As has been earlier noted, C-A sections on all floors have closed ventilation systems.

On day three of the initial presentation of the original patient, the decision was made to amputate the extremities—again, not because of bacterial infection but because of necrotic gangrene. (Until then, possible alternate diagnoses of swine flu and avian flu had been entertained, thoroughly discussed, and then discarded.)

Dr. Todd McGuire performed the amputations on the first patient and, again, on the following day, on the second.

The mother, or patient three, exhibited severe signs of emotional distress and was administered Xanax.

"Stories" were developed in committee and by consensus to explain the whereabouts of the—by now, seven—missing members of the medical staff. Staffers were encouraged to phone home (using their cell phones) as often as seemed appropriate. Every emphasis possible was placed on remaining calm.

The sisters were brave in their distress. They underwent extensive questioning as to their whereabouts in the past month but were unable to give any useful information. They had not traveled to any foreign countries; they had attended no sports events, and had been to few restaurants or films. To this date no one else in the city, to our knowledge, has presented with these symptoms. There is, however, always the possibility that others have fallen ill and have been kept at home.

On days four and five respectively, the sisters expired. The bodies were removed and cremated at Westwood Mortuary. Confidentiality agreements were drawn up and signed. The family continues under quarantine. The mother remains under sedation.

Questions have arisen from this event. How many patients can the Medical Center's C-A sections accommodate, not theoretically but in actuality? How many mortuaries should be privy to unexpected medical events? Keeping in mind the media frenzy connected with the original SARS epidemic in 2003, how much secrecy should be striven for, or is an open press the more desirable option?

More salient questions remain: Were these cases mere medical anomalies, random events that occur once in a decade or a lifetime? Were they, perhaps, part of a "trial run" from an outside hostile source? Or could they have been part of our own security efforts (admittedly crude), a method of testing our own swift response?

It should be said that the Medical Center performed well during this trying time, but these were only two cases.

A diagnosis has not yet been made. Tissue tests are going forward in the C-A lab on floor six.

Sincerely,
Philip Fuchs, MD

The girls had wept from the very beginning. They'd been in terrible pain, unable to swallow, doubled up by stomach cramps, burning with fever. You could barely see their poor fingers; the palms lapped out and over them. When the skin broke, the stench was awful. That was when they'd had to take the mother out, using a trick from bad movies: an injection given by one nurse while another nurse held her immobile.

She was in restraints now, until somebody figured out what they were going to do next. But nobody knew what they were going to do next. The mortuary people hadn't been happy. If it was bad enough to be secret, bad enough to kill you, they didn't want to be part of it. And what he'd tried to say in the next to last paragraph—sure, they'd managed pretty well, extremely well, but these were just two people sick and dying. What if it turned out to be two thousand or two million?

What was it? That was the thing, what was it? Not his job, thank God. And no other cases like them. But he was going to have to tell the mother. And then step back and let some government goon threaten her. And then go home. He'd been away less than a week.

They'd been pretty and flirtatious even as they wept. That first day even the sick one was tan and blond and confident and cute. They dashed their bangs out of their eyes and then said *ouch* because their hands hurt, even then. They knew, they took it for granted, that there would be some antibiotic they'd take and be right out on the beach again.

He wished he knew who was behind Colonel Robert Davies. He wished he could check this with Davenport, but he was writing a separate report.

Of course, it could be nothing. People died all the time. Maybe they'd eaten something toxic. Or it might have been a household chemical. He'd been told not to speculate. (But he had.) He'd even seen an in-house e-mail that called this event a possibly "fortuitous occurrence," a "test case in the best sense."

But they were just girls from Silver Lake, little girls, fifteen and seventeen years old.

He read the report over and added, *The cause of death was systemic organ failure.*

Now he was looking at a shower, a shave, a trip to the outside, which he hadn't seen in six days, and the ride home. His wife had told him to stop at Gelson's.

"I know I'm not supposed to ask you anything."

He put two bags down on the counter. "I got salmon. Corn on the cob. Heirloom tomatoes. Olive oil—a new kind."

"Salmon has mercury. Didn't you see the sign about it on the fish counter? Nothing too bad happened, did it? Or wouldn't you still be there? Was it just a drill? I know you can't tell me."

"Only if you're pregnant. That's the only real danger with mercury."

"Yes," she said restlessly, "but you know, I might be. I might *get* pregnant. I know what you said, but I don't want to rule anything out. If it were something more serious, you'd tell me, wouldn't you?"

"I'd tell you."

"But men lie. I mean, if you were having an affair you certainly wouldn't tell me that. Would you? Except if you got caught?"

"I wouldn't have an affair. I'm not having an affair. For God's sake!"

He left the kitchen, went into the den, under the dark stairway, into the bar. Opened a bottle of Steerforth.

"Phil! It's the morning! It's not even eleven o'clock."

"Why don't you join me," he said. "What the hell. I'm off work. You don't have anything to do. Let's go outside. Give me a break on this."

"I was all *alone,* Phil. You don't know what it's like."

He knew the wine should breathe but he didn't care, he couldn't wait. He took two hefty swallows and poured some more. "Want some?"

"It's not even noon." She stood in the doorway of the bar, between him and the light.

"Ah, Felicia!"

But she pulled back. "What was it? Was it contagious? I have a right to know. I have my children to look out for."

"Couldn't we"—he groped for words—"couldn't we not live our lives out of the funny papers?"

She eyed him. "I don't know what you mean. Did you get any sleep in there? I don't like the way you're acting. You have to tell me, because I'm going to find out anyway. And you have an obligation to us. An obligation to the kids. Should we leave the city? God knows, I've begged you to do it! Can't you at least tell me that?"

"Nobody is leaving any city. I'm beat. I'm going to lie down."

"You haven't even asked about the kids."

"Felicia. What about the kids?"

"They were worried! I was too. I don't like you being gone like this."

"I need to lie down."

"You're sure it was nothing to worry about?"

He took his glass and bottle, headed upstairs. She followed him.

It was a beautiful morning. Leaves swayed dizzily up against the windowpanes of their master bedroom.

"Where *are* they? The kids?"

"At school, of course."

He pulled off his shoes and socks, lay back, patted her side of the bed. "Come here. Lie down with me."

She did, propped up on her elbow. "I went ahead with the membership. I really *do* want to celebrate my birthday. Because— the way things are going!"

He was so tired.

"I mean, all this is contingent on . . . everything being OK? You'd tell me, you really *would* tell me, if everything wasn't OK?"

"Can we talk about something else? Why don't you come over here? Put your head on my shoulder."

Hesitantly she inched her way over toward him. "I just want *everything* to be OK. You've always tried to be good to me. I do know that."

Sleepy, he'd never been so sleepy. But it was always that way with them. Maybe with everybody. When one person wanted to talk the other didn't. Maybe it was just as well.

"I've been thinking. When you were gone. If there are four people in a house, then you should divide up everything four ways in the house. And maybe the kids deserve a bonus because they're kids."

His fingers began to tingle. Just one of those somatic things. Funny, he hadn't felt much fear when it was going on. It was nice to know that about himself.

"But we can't count *ourselves* out either. Especially in times like this, do you know what I mean? Nobody knows what's going to happen next. So we owe it to ourselves to do what it is that we think is best for ourselves? Because we only have our one life? And what if there isn't a God? What if there's nothing after? Just what we have and just what we've done? And if we haven't done what we think is best for own selves, then we won't have done what's best for ourselves. You know?"

He reached out and took her hand. So small and fine boned. "You little monkey," he said.

"So I want to be in the club. And I want a party. And I bought an air filter for the house, in case there really is an epidemic. Or a bomb? And it's good for allergies. So it's good for the kids."

It was a warm, soft, familiar feeling from his childhood. *Could we all lie down on the big bed?* The darkness danced all around him. And maybe it was his mother—back when she was happy—who he felt quietly padding through the dim room while he had his nap. While she removed something from his fingers. And silently encouraged him to go on sleeping.

PHIL

Janet, Phil's mother-in-law, was the best that money could buy. Body-lifted and buffed by daily Pilates, dressed in unimpeachable violet, smarter than her daughter by a long shot, smarter than her husband, Al, certainly smarter than Phil. He couldn't hold it against her, because she was kind. Janet put others first and it wasn't a scam. He'd seen her empty her wallet for a homeless woman on the Promenade. He'd seen her take off her jacket and give it to a shivering child. A world away from his own mom.

Janet adored her daughter and her grandchildren and they were foiled by her; she was simply too sweet, too good, too beautiful and smart to be made fun of. To be rude to. He couldn't be mean to her either, even if he'd wanted to be, because—against all odds—out of the whole bunch of that side of the family and his, he knew she loved him.

They met for lunch down at the Palomino. What a mom! Nothing like *his* mother, who passed her time sulking or criticizing, bemoaning the plight of the widow lady and all the injustice of the world.

But Janet looked pensive today, a little drawn. She'd ordered some white wine, and her carefully smooth forehead was creased with concern.

"I wanted you to help me with the guest list for Felicia's party. I'm not sure I know the best people to ask. You look tired, Phil. I hope I'm not—"

"Oh . . . no. I just don't see why you and she can't take care of it. Felicia's the one who knows everyone we know. But don't worry about it! I always like to see you." He ordered a gin and tonic. "And it's good to get away from work."

"To tell you the truth, I'm just a little bit worried about Felicia. I wonder if I've done anything to offend her?"

"How could you?"

"I don't know. But usually we talk every day. Now she's either not home or she's not picking up. And when I do get her—well, you know. Sometimes she gets sad. I just hope it's not something I did. That's one reason the party might be a good idea. To . . . you know—"

"Snap her out of it?"

"I guess."

He sighed, and drank.

"She does get this way sometimes," Janet said. "A little sad. In the fall. Sometimes I think it could be light deprivation."

"Yeah, but we live in *Southern California*! And what is it— *May*, right now?"

She laughed. "So, we thought about fifty people?"

"I'm not sure we know fifty people."

"Al and me. You and Felicia. Eloise and Vernon. And suppose we say they can each have two friends? That's ten right there. And your mother, of course."

"Janet, she wants a baby. That's one of the problems."

His mother-in-law hesitated. "It's hard. It's hard for all of us. It's about getting older. You know, Phil, I know you'd never do it, but you're right around the age where you might think of leaving and getting yourself a trophy wife and having another couple of kids. I don't think she wants—"

"Like I'm going to get a trophy wife. Jesus! Where am I going to pick her up, the trophy store?"

"I'm not saying it has anything to do with reality. I just think she doesn't want to be the *old* wife. I think she wants to be the *new* wife. I shouldn't be talking this way. It's presumptuous. But nobody likes to get older. I think that's what it is."

"*Tell* me!"

"So. I know Felicia wants Tracy and Lisa and Jeanette and Margie and Rita and Patricia and their husbands, and she's already given me their addresses. What about you?"

He gave her the names and addresses of Jack and his wife and

a couple of other guys on staff. And his mother, of course. Together they thought of a few single people—divorced people—
balancing them into couples. They weren't going to get to fifty
today. "I'm *sorry,*" he said irritably. "I do the best I can, I really do,
but I'm not Mr. Social."

"What about Larry?"

"What *about* him?"

"I think Felicia might like him to come."

"He's an asshole!"

"I think she might like him to come."

"I don't get it. Really."

"She gets these ideas—*you* know, that like there's some other
whole world that she, not that she missed *out,* but that she—
I can't explain it."

"Hey. It's OK with me. It's not my party."

She smiled at him. "What would you do? If it were your
party?"

He had an immediate vision of a large, large lake. Something
like Big Bear Lake only bigger. Maybe the ocean. Maybe the Pacific. A rowboat. He and Vernon. Maybe fishing, maybe not. But
not a sound in the world to be heard.

"I don't know. Get out on the water someplace?"

She smiled, teasing him. "A luxury yacht? Caviar? Dancing?
That reminds me. She wants live music. She wants to dance."

"Whatever."

"And we have to pick the menu."

"Can't you guys do that? I don't know anything about it. Anything I pick she's going to hate!"

He saw the faintest hint of Felicia's perpetually discontented expression. "Of course she can do it. But she wants *us* to do it, *you* to do it. Because it would mean you're thinking of her."

"I *am* thinking of her! I *do* think of her! I'm here right now, aren't I?"

"Of course."

"What about salmon? Some kind of salad? Some kind of pasta? A cake with her name on it? Speeches? Is that what she wants?"

"Passed hors d'oeuvres? Beforehand?"

He felt a wave of despair.

"Sure. Sure. Absolutely."

"So. Are you busy at the Medical Center?"

"Yeah. We've been doing a lot of training for civil emergencies. Nobody knows what they're doing. It's been pretty hairy."

"Felicia says you're doing extra work."

He looked at her. "You want to know if I had a hard day at the office, dear?"

"Seriously."

"Seriously, I think they're scared shitless—sorry—about security. They think something's coming and they don't have a clue. They're waiting for somebody else to figure something out."

"Do you talk to Felicia about it?"

He laughed. "Are you kidding me? No!"

"Doesn't she deserve to know your feelings about this?"

He wanted to say, She's already as crazy as a Mason jar full of spiders, but he didn't. He said, "She's under enough pressure as it is. The kids are a handful right now."

Blah blah blah.

She looked at him directly. "It's a scary time. For everyone, I think."

"Yes, it is."

PHIL

Felicia had gone over to the club earlier, working on the place cards and table plans she'd been changing around for weeks. She'd been obsessing for days, buying dresses, sending them back, driving the chef at the club—as far as Phil could tell from the one-sided phone calls he picked up on—absolutely nuts.

This evening around five she'd shimmied into what she'd finally picked out to wear, something green that left her back and arms bare. "Do I look OK? I think this is the best dress I've ever had. Do you like it? Isn't it wonderful?"

The sun hadn't gone down yet; it slanted into their master bedroom, glinting off the taffeta of their king-sized bed, picking up every little wrinkle on her powdered face. She was too old to wear a dress like that.

"You look great, babe."

He'd disappointed her. She went back to the mirror. He had to stop himself from sighing. Maybe he sighed anyway.

Eloise came in. She was hardly talking to either of them. If anything, she seemed more ticked at her mother than at him.

"Didn't you say we were *leaving* by now? Didn't you tell them we'd be there before six?"

His daughter looked great but she was dressed like a whore. Plenty of straps and fuck-me sandals. Again, he held back a sigh. But Eloise could have cared less what he thought.

After they left he went down to the den, opened some wine, watched the five o'clock news. Chemical weapons, another SARS-like case in Malaysia that sent the stock market down, flu in northern Europe, bubonic plague in one of the stans— Tajikistan?—pneumonia in Egypt, another chase on the 405, with the driver holding a gun to his own head. That security-level thing gone up a notch again, but they wouldn't say why.

Phil went to the door of the den and yelled up. "Vern? *Vern!*"

"YEAH?"

"Be sure you're getting ready. We have to leave by six thirty."

Cocktails at seven, dinner at eight, dancing nine thirty to eleven thirty. Home by midnight if he was lucky.

"Vern?"

"WHAT!"

Phil sat back down, poured some more wine. What was he worrying about, the world or his wife? Did he give a shit? There was nothing he could do about anything. Maybe it would get better when the kids were grown and out of the house. World peace might happen.

Or maybe not. Probably not.

He had to tie Vern's tie. The kid was right out of the shower, soft and pink. He looked like he'd just woken up from a long nap. . . .

Now Vern sat in the car and looked . . . cagey. Or maybe caged. High on pot? Or was it something else? Bad wiring in his brain? Or just that bad stage. Or maybe he hated all this as much as Phil did.

Phil drew in his breath. Vern moved his left hand. That was the end of that conversation.

Dinner was out on the club veranda, taking advantage of bright spring weather. Other members looked warily at them, taking in the tuxes. Old folks, not coming to their party, huddled together on sofas in the main room and dined elsewhere.

From downstairs he could faintly hear hectic rhythms from the fitness rooms. Those people never gave up.

Four courses, was that it? Salad with arugula and feta cheese, sand dabs—a hell of a lot more expensive than salmon!—baby vegetables, dessert. Sorbet and melon before the cake. Plenty of good wine. *Dad?* He addressed either or both of them. *I'm giving a dinner for what turned out to be seventy people. With live dancing.*

His dads didn't answer.

Felicia and Eloise paced by the tables. Checking out the flowers. Making sure the outdoor heaters worked. Conferring with the maître d'. Phil passed them by, went over to the veranda railing, looked down onto lighted tennis courts. Two old guys at the far end banged balls back and forth. Rallying. Killing time.

Then people started coming. Funny how the tuxes did it, dressed things up. Women always managed to look pretty good but men needed something drastic. A tux or a white dinner jacket. Far better than a good suit.

When Eloise's friends started coming in, the air lightened. Pretty girls, dithering. Felicia went into hostess mode and he guessed he was the host, pumping hands, hugging the women, jabbing guys in their arms. The musicians tuned up and began. A regular party.

Felicia, whispering like a teenager into her girlfriend's ear. Her girlfriend nodding earnestly, encouragingly. The passed hors d'oeuvres began.

When had salad started to have feta cheese on it? How about that balsamic stuff? One thing, food had gotten better in the last twenty years.

The sand dabs were overdone, but they were his grand gesture.

His cell phone rang. The number was Hospital Emergency.

"We've got something. Masks and the isolation room. No, don't come in. We're informing staff as a precaution: 134, 134."

In the wrong line of work. He was in the wrong line of work. He poured another glass, felt Felicia looking at him. What the hell. He'd paid for it.

Melon balls. His mother used to make melon balls. Here they

were again. His mother also made those great sandwiches—cream cheese and maraschino cherries, chopped up fine. Then she trimmed the crusts. Sweet sandwiches, she called them. Pink sandwiches. When she was with Charlie and she was pretty happy. Tonight she sat across the room, gamely making conversation with somebody. She didn't like Felicia. Never had.

Speeches. He got up and gave one himself. Wonderful friends. Wonderful family. Two beautiful women. Wonderful son. Couldn't be more lucky.

Round of applause. Not bad at all.

Then, dancing. He didn't like it but he did it. Felt his tie get tweaked. Felt Felicia's muscles twitching under the green cloth.

"Are you spazzing?" he asked. Because she had lots of trouble with her back.

"You need a relaxant?" Because he always carried them.

He'd disappointed her again. Well, fuck it.

He ducked into the smoking room for a cigar. Ten forty-five. Went back to the dancing. Found Eloise talking to her friends.

"Have you seen your mother?"

She shrugged.

"How about Vern?"

Rolled her eyes.

Someday, Missy . . .

But he didn't say it.

He went out onto the far side of the veranda away from the noisy band. The old guys playing tennis had hung it up and gone home. Should he go down to the Med Center? Or was it that he'd do anything to get out of here?

Something moved out there in the dark at the far end of the veranda. He knew what it was before he knew it. Some crummy drama. Mr. Tall-Dark-and-Debonair. Larry. A swish of something green and sheer.

"Oh, Phil. I didn't want you to find out this way!"

The hell you didn't.

He went all through the club, looking for Vern. Found him where he thought he might, in the fitness room, pumping the crap out of a stationary bicycle, tie pulled off, studs off, streaming sweat.

"Kid. Have you been down here the whole time?"

"So did you see it? DID YOU FINALLY SEE IT?"

"Yes," he said. "I did."

Vern got off the bike and ran, locking his arms around Phil's waist. "Finally," he sobbed. "Finally."

Behind Phil came his mother's voice. "I knew something like this was happening. That damned stupid slut."

PHIL

It was hot: hot brush-fire weather. The rains hadn't come this winter. In late May, arsonists from San Diego to above Point Conception torched ryegrass—a three-hundred-mile fire line. It burned through Topanga and down through Malibu and gave Santa Barbara and San Diego and even Los Angeles runs for their money. The fires looked to have been set simultaneously. So, was it Muslim fanatics? Ecoterrorists? Or just plain arsonists? It didn't matter much to those families, half the length of the state, photographed glumly surveying their domestic ruins.

And the fevers that flared up all over the southern part of the state after that, serious but rarely fatal—were they a variant of San Joaquin, the fungus that came from turned-over raw dirt and killed a few dozen unfortunate migrant workers every year? Or something animal-borne like SARS or avian flu? Phil woke up in the night, thinking of it. He was no epidemiologist, certainly, but he knew more by now than he'd ever wanted to know. The rash that came with the fever, the hardening of the glands under the arms, the nosebleeds—it looked, if such a thing were possible, like a "light" case of the plague. Certainly, enough rodents in the scorched hills around LA had died or fled to make the plague possible. Wasn't that how the 1926 flare-up had started? No, that had been a ship from Mexico landing at San Pedro from—where?—Manzanillo? Mazatlán? One thing from his infectious disease class long ago that he'd never forget: those people got off the boat and drove to a boardinghouse in downtown LA, and by the following Monday everyone in the house was dead, with the cabdriver thrown in for good measure. Just one kid in a crib survived. That's how fast it could spread. That was right here, he thought, less than a hundred years ago. It could happen again.

But were there *ever* light cases of something like that? Would it be to someone's advantage to engineer something debilitating but not fatal? Sure. Because then retaliation would be delayed. Because suppose there was nothing real to retaliate against?

Not that anybody ever asked him. He was just called in to verify the rash.

Then, another variant of symptoms, another fever, another sort of rash, began to show up. Over 90 percent of the "victims" were women and girls. This one presented as a major allergic reaction (which didn't, however, respond to antihistamines). The fever was high, accompanied by nasal swelling and congestion of the throat. No bacterial or virological connections could be pinned down. A couple of children died, and it took the press about a week to figure out the common denominator. Mawkish stories about "shopping with Mommy" appeared and were repeated, and a cluster of sick salesgirls down for the count narrowed it down. Somebody traced whatever it was to perfume atomizers on the main floors of department stores.

Or not.

The time between living together and living apart was something else Phil thought about now. Couldn't a couple just break up and be done with it? But no. He couldn't leave until he'd said everything he'd had to say: *How could she?* And (he knew it didn't make him look good) how could she have done all of it on *his* dime, at a party *he'd* paid for, that he hadn't wanted to have, a celebration that made *him* look like a fool—no, a cuckold? *In front of their friends?* How could she have done it? And of course the kids had known, which explained what *they'd* been doing for the last six months!

To which she got to answer—at the top of her voice, and repeatedly—that it was the only way to get his attention, that she was sick and tired of being cast aside or ignored, that her life counted for something too . . . until Vern pounded on their bedroom door, screaming "SHUT UP, SHUT UP!" and Eloise went to stay for a couple of weeks at a girlfriend's house while her parents went at it some more.

He knew he'd have to move out, but the only one who knew how to take care of that stuff was Felicia; he couldn't stop, in the middle of yelling (or *her* yelling) and say, "I really need a place here on the west side, not too close to the beach, two bedrooms would be best, and it doesn't have to have a pool. Do you think you could find one for me?" No, because she'd already be pulling out all the stops: "If I could only have had a child, another child, something just for *me,* but no, you were too selfish; it was all about you and how you'd be *inconvenienced!*" Strange how there were rules in the most wild-and-woolly knock-down drag-out fights, because the one time he did say, almost without thinking about it, "Hey! I didn't not *let* you do something. You could have stopped taking the pill. Not wore your diaphragm. Whatever it is you use," she drew in an enraged, truly startled breath and went at his face with her fingernails.

Still, in those weeks, he went home at night, didn't know what else to do. And she cooked for him: braised shrimp in olive oil and garlic, that swordfish of hers, vegetable curries, sometimes chicken in sherry and cream, even though it was against both their diets. *Eat it and weep,* she said to him silently, and then later, at the top of her voice. And he did.

On Saturdays after those training sessions, he began going through his things, throwing stuff away. If he was going to live in an apartment, where would he put his undergraduate textbooks, the paper he got an A on in Philosophy, the golf trophy he ended up with once, his old shirts, the stamp collection from when he was a kid? It got so that Phil made the drive to the Salvation Army almost as easily as he went to work.

And then came the night when he pushed Felicia, gave her a little shove, and she yelled at the top of her voice, *again,* "*Don't!* I know you don't care about me, but you'll hurt the *baby!*"

Baby?

The school year ended a week early because of "security concerns." Vern still didn't have a school to go to next fall. Everywhere Phil went, WASH YOUR HANDS warned him. Stores and restaurants were almost empty. He would have talked to Felicia about this, but they weren't really talking.

He got a call one Sunday afternoon from the Med Center. Eleven new cases. Of something. No deaths yet. But along the inside walls of the building there was new art, old posters mocked up from World War II: LOOSE LIPS SINK SHIPS! He knew it was no coincidence. And when a reporter called him at home to ask "off the record" about the rashes that went with these new fevers, Phil knew enough, remembering the rainbow of cherries and olives and onions that had flown through the bar of the Palomino, to say that it was summer, wasn't it? Every late spring in Southern California took its toll in respiratory diseases. Because the weather was hot, unseasonably hot. And shouldn't the reporter be calling the press person at the hospital?

During his theatricals with Felicia, he remembered to grunt out to her that she ought to keep the kids out of public places as much as she could, and although she answered, at the top of her voice, "Of course, *them*! Not that you would ever think about *me*!" he could see she noticed, and presumably she did something about it.

He came home early one evening to find her pouring boiling water over fresh vegetables. "Good girl," he said, and she shrugged and looked away.

They had to do something. If she was pregnant it probably

wasn't his. But what if it was? What was he supposed to do, ask for one of those tests? Because it had to be Larry's. (And just to thicken the plot, Phil and Felicia had sex, more now than in a long time. *Fuck me and weep,* he thought the message was, just like with dinner.)

On May 28, three deaths got reported, downtown, over at King Drew Medical. Respiratory, with accompanying rashes. The victims were Hispanic. Illegal, probably. *La Opinión* ran the story but suggested it was bad oysters. *Ostiones* from the gulf, poisoned by warm waters. On May 29, Phil saw two cases of something at UCLA on respirators. He was called in to verify and record the rash. It looked like smallpox to him, but what did he know about smallpox? He'd never seen the real thing. The place was crawling with Feds and reporters who didn't look like reporters, all asking his mom in the main lobby if she couldn't tell them something off the record. Behind her desk, behind the florist shop and the gift shop, before where the business part of the Medical Center began, a half dozen workers were setting up a wrought-iron latticelike thing that would come together at night—clank—and lock.

In the car his cell phone rang and Felicia asked if he could come home early. She'd been listening to the radio, and her voice was jittery with hysteria. He said no, he was still working.

He hadn't said *smallpox.* He'd said, "Deep acute subcutaneous abrasions." He'd already had the vaccination, along with some other stuff. He phoned Felicia back. "I'll be staying at a hotel a few days. At the Miramar, probably. I'll be calling you. You can have Larry over if you want to." He hung up before she could say anything.

Then he called right back and blurted out, "Don't worry," and hung up again.

He sat in his parked car and read a feature story in the *Times* about Americans moving in droves to Brazil and Argentina "to pursue a more relaxed, less stressful way of life."

Then he called the colonel on his cell phone.

"I'm out," Phil said. "I can't do this anymore. Something has come up. I'm having domestic problems."

"The hell you are, soldier!"

"I'm not a soldier. I can't do it."

"You've got the training. You've got the know-how. We're looking at a possible national emergency here. Understand, I emphasize the word *possible*."

"I can't," Phil said again. "I have family emergencies."

"Get it through your head. You're not going anywhere."

PHIL and EDITH

Phil drove.

His mother sat beside him in the passenger seat, peering closely at her list of addresses, written in her own hand. They inched down San Vicente toward the ocean. It was a beautiful day, a fine afternoon. The June fog had burned off early, leaving a misty softness over the trees and lawn that divided the street. Runners glided smoothly down the strip. Over here on the north side, the weekly Sunday San Vicente car sale was in business—a string of half a dozen or so collector's items with their owners lounging idly next to them. Just a way to get out of the house, Phil thought. They didn't want to sell those cars, they just wanted to see and be seen, be part of the collecting elite.

"Make a turn here," said his mother. "It's over on the other side."

He slowed, waited for a break in the strip, turned back, and headed east, looking for 14447½. Here it was, lemon yellow, two-story, built in a U, three sides facing a courtyard that was just grass, a way that apartment dwellers could at least catch sight of a respectable patch of green.

"Two bedrooms, two baths, built-in appliances, den. Access to gym."

"That's awfully small."

"You'll be living alone, Phil! You're telling me you want two separate rooms for when the kids come over?"

He thought of himself, rattling around in an apartment, spending interminable weekends with Vern, with Eloise. Eloise! Rolling her eyes and saying *Whatever!* Or just rolling her eyes. Slamming the door. Laughing at him on the cell phone with her girlfriend while he sat on a couch in the living room, looking out on that patch of green.

"Two bedrooms. That's OK, I guess."

Still, he couldn't move.

"Come on. Let's take a look at it."

She got out of the car and stood, waiting for him.

"There's no sidewalk here."

She took a breath, thought better of what she was going to say, and waited until she had another new paragraph.

"Won't you be coming in from behind, in the alley, where the parking is? You won't really be needing a sidewalk, do you think?"

"I was just saying. Just thinking."

"It's only an apartment. Until you decide what you're going to be doing. You don't have to stay there forever! Come on. Let's at least go in."

What could he do but follow her as she trudged off across the lawn? He was lucky she'd offered to go with him, find the listings, talk to the managers, all that. It was what Felicia would have done in better days. He couldn't ask any of his friends because now he didn't much trust them, except for Jack. What if they'd known all along about Felicia? Come to think of it, what if they'd known about *him*?

He hated this. Hated it!

The apartment was open this afternoon. And they weren't the only lookers. He recognized the strict, blood-draining gleam of Navajo White, a thick coat of the stuff on every wall. The place reeked of it. And new, gray, faintly industrial carpeting over everything. Tacky crystal chandeliers in every room except the bathroom. A breakfast nook. The dining-room part of the living room. Small windows. Both bedrooms overlooked the alley, and the apartment house across the alley, and all the cars parked in their silly little slots. The other apartment house had little balconies that overlooked this same alley, balconies stuffed with potted plants and bikes and miniature hibachis and quantities of white plastic furniture.

"I don't like it," he said loudly to his mother. "Besides, it's too much money."

They'd been driving for a while again, looking for the next address on this street, when his mother spoke up. "You know, you can't afford to be picky in this market. There's almost nothing out here; I think I already told you that. And you don't want to buy a condo until after the settlement, or she'll do her best to take it, along with everything else."

"She won't take it. She'd never *take* it."

Silence. Just the sound of his mother breathing. It sounded like she was doing it deliberately, clammed up, keeping her temper.

"So. Where do we go next?"

"We keep going in this direction. Back toward Brentwood."

The next building was pink, with a circular asphalt driveway and a pool where the courtyard might have been. Hardwood floors, tiny rooms. Navajo White, glaring away.

"Too small," Phil said.

And the next, a guesthouse behind a mansion above Sunset. Only one bedroom and a smell of cigarettes and mold.

"I'm not an undergraduate," Phil said, "I'm a doctor. I've already been through this stage."

His mother muttered something.

"What?"

"Then *act* like it, for God's sake! Act like a grown-up for once!"

Again they were in the car. His mother looked out the window.

"OK," he said. "Where to?"

The drive took them down to Venice. It was an apartment, all right, but it had been carved out of someone's old house. Plants of every kind covered everything in sight. Overgrown. Neglected. They didn't bother to go in, just peered from the driveway. He didn't say anything, just looked at her.

"It isn't my fault," she said irritably. "I didn't get in this mess, you did!"

He didn't answer, just went back to the car. They'd never find a place at this rate, and he didn't know why that pleased him. Maybe something like: *See: It's not so easy, life! It's not as easy as everyone makes it out to be.*

But she had his number, of course.

"Look, Phil, I'm sorry. I know she's a bitch. I've always said it. Maybe not to you, but I've said it! She was— I know it's a cliché, but she was never good enough for you and this proves it. She's a lying slut, but that doesn't change or *impinge upon in any way* the fact that you've got to get out of there! The more you put it off the worse it's going to be, and it's not doing the kids any good either. They'll think you'll put up with it like you put up with everything, but she's a slut besides being a moron, and you've got to show some determination. Otherwise, you're just putting up with adultery. They've got a name for that. They've got all kinds of names."

"It's not about that, really," he said. "I mean, I had somebody for a while too. It's that she paraded it around in front of the kids. She messed with their minds. Just to get my attention, she says."

She took it in. Took a breath and sighed it out. "She probably would have hired a blimp if she could, to get your attention. I *get* it. But what are you going to do now? Are you really going to stay? Or are you going to go? And when are you going to *decide*?"

"She's really not that bad, Ma."

But she wouldn't give on that one. "I never liked that woman," Edith said. "For my money, she's a moron. But it's none of my business. You do what you want."

"I will," he said. "I guess."

They had one more stop, back on San Vicente. His mother said she'd wanted to make it a circular drive. This place was yellow, a couple was still living in it, and the furniture made it seem almost human. It wouldn't be available for four months. That sounded right to him. A way of satisfying everyone, maybe.

"I'll take it," he said, gave over a bunch of references, showed his faculty ID card, signed something on the spot. He figured his mom was on to him, mentally shaking her head again over his spinelessness, his procrastination, but she kept her mouth shut.

Back in the car, she took another breath and he braced for what she'd say. What he heard was mild and sad.

"You're a good man, Phil. I know you'll do what's best for everyone. I'm sorry this has happened, I really am."

EDITH

There comes a time when you can't avoid it. Or you can't keep doing what you have been doing. It's not because of lack of energy, at least I don't think so. It might be despair, finally setting in. Despair, different from grief and a big sin, as I seem to remember.

It comes on around six at night. Because you have lunch with your friends and then you go shopping and then you take yourself for a drink—no matter what Phil says!—but then, unless you want to go to a movie alone, you're looking at going home. Or even after a day at the Med Center (which I have to say I'm grateful for), there's the drive home. And opening the door, into the apartment. And all you can hear is some ringing in your ears. And it's five hours before you can decently even think of sleeping.

You look at the walls and think about it. And you turn on the television and the news is not only awful but boring, so that you want to say to those strutting idiots, *Go ahead, if you want to so much!* Bomb everyone you can find into smithereens, women and children first and put the rest in jail, and I'm talking every last one of us, so then at least we won't have to listen to your lies and watch your dreadful smirking faces!

And I think, *If I only had some company,* but my company is gone. The play I acted in is about to close; my stars and supporting actors are dead or dying. Except for Phil, I think, and I get almost physically sick, thinking of him somewhere in a hotel, and I can't even hate Felicia—it's not her fault, really. It's a great life if you don't weaken, but what if you do? Felicia weakened. Phil calls me when he has the time. And if I were a different kind of person, I'd call Eloise and say *Let's go shopping*! but I can't stand her attitude. Or I'd call Vernon and say—my God, I don't know what I'd say. I'm sixty-four, he's eleven.

So this is how I'd been feeling for about a month: alone, alone, alone. And when I thought of the war, of the terrorists, I could only think, Nobody will even look for me until a month goes by! And the last person I could talk to about any of this was Melinda Barclay, because—*boy!*—she had the look on her, and I had it on me. It was like one cancer patient sizing up another.

So I was in a dark frame of mind when in June a manila envelope came in the mail. I recognized the handwriting and the return address. The letter was written on full-sized eight-by-eleven-inch paper, both sides. It had been carefully planned, one page about the loss of my husband and the years gone by, and on the next page a prudent amount of news about himself. On a sep-arate stiffer page, a collage of the kind he used to love to make, a series of photographs of his seventieth birthday party. On a thin-ner piece of tracing paper, he'd labeled all the relatives: his aunts and uncles and his children, so much older now than when I'd first met them. All adults.

After three or four days, he called me. What bravery, really.

We made a date to meet for drinks the next afternoon at the Palomino, after I finished my shift. I wouldn't put it past him to stand me up, because as I remembered I might have broken up with him a thousand years ago.

I saw an old guy in a windbreaker, a scarf, and one of those floppy canvas hats walking south on Galey. He stopped for a sig-nal and looked both ways. It wasn't fair that I could watch him that way from the safety of the restaurant. Then he was across the street and inside and coming my way. He was smiling.

He looked like manna in the desert.

If somebody came by now, I thought, they'd think it was just two people drinking in the afternoon. Both a little short and old. Of no importance in the greater scheme of things. Or even the smaller scheme of things. Somebody did come by, and I ordered another drink.

"Well," I said finally, "if we ever do really go out—"

"What do you think that collage was for? That was a two-page *letter* there! Don't you think that's enough of a presentation?"

Yeah, I thought. Yes. Certainly. But don't you think I know you've got stacks of those collages around the house?

He was funny with words. Not recordably funny, not monumental. He called the president a pusillanimous pussy, for the pure dumb pleasure of lining up those *p*'s. So for a week I was happy.

I still had other worries, like everybody else. I made sure I bought candles, and canned goods that wouldn't be too disgusting if you had to eat them cold, if the war finally "came home," like some philandering husband. Every time I went shopping I bought drinking water—one gallon—and one bottle of champagne, because if half of what they said was going to happen really did happen, I knew I'd want champagne and the hell with the drinking water. He couldn't have cared less about any of it.

One night we strolled across a park to a little café on the Palisades, talking about nothing. What an odd sensation *that* was! Something more to tell my friend Melinda about. Here was the past, the skinny palms against navy blue sky, the sound of the same old ocean blending with the traffic on the avenue, and here was the restaurant we were going to now, made into a new hokey place with king crab and ribs.

"Aw," the waitress said, when we came in, as in *Aw, that's cute*!

But the next night, around six o'clock, the phone rang. "About dinner," he said, "I'm afraid I can't make it. Can you take a rain check?"

The sounds of a party echoed behind him. A lot of people talking.

"No worries," I said, but I was stung. I liked him a lot. Needed him, goddamm it.

"I had a heart attack. I'm calling from the emergency room at UCLA."

"I'm sorry," I said. I didn't believe a word of it.

"About an hour ago. I called nine-one-one. They brought me to UCLA. *Your* hangout."

"On a scale of one to ten, what's your pain?" a rude voice cut in, and he answered, impatient, "Seven."

I sat in my living room in a nice dress and watched the night open up. Because I *so much* didn't want to go over there. Go through it again.

I compromised by calling the volunteer desk, telling some other lady she could go home and telling her why.

But I was right when I thought it sounded like a party. When I got there, I saw a lot of people and heard a lot of excited talk.

"When you *really* think about it," one passing intern said to another, "where do you draw the line between *chemical* and *biological*?"

The Chinese family finally got it that night that their uncle was, really was, brain-dead. It looked like plug-pulling night for them. They cried.

I could have gone upstairs and seen my friend, but I didn't have the guts. I couldn't go through it again.

I sat in my chair at the information desk and thought about the information I'd learned since I came here to volunteer. The rumors.

They say that anthrax—remember the whole anthrax scare?—was a government plot, it turns out, hatched at Johns Hopkins. They'd been planning it for years in strictest secrecy and seized the moments after 9/11 to play it out. They say. And they say that's how the cats got killed here: a kind of anthrax that spread to the cats, and we were just damn lucky.

They say that over in the Jules Stein Clinic they've made blind men see. They say that's a "security" experiment too, part of all those night vision goggles they use in desert wars, just taken one step further. They say the blind men can't let on what happened; it's still a big secret. The blind men can go home from the clinic, but they have to carry their white canes and look pitiful. They can't even tell their wives. (But isn't that always the way?)

They say that somewhere in this building the bodies of the brain-dead homeless are kept alive strung up to machines, a lending library of organs. They say lots of our organs come from across the sea, but I don't really believe it.

They say that son of mine has either been hacking into the kidney waiting list or he's asking around about medical cocaine or he's part of an elite cadre fighting terrorism. I just have to shake my head.

And they say there's a gangster—or some kind of undercover man, or a government man?—who *really* needs his looks changed, that he's being medically scalped and given an entire face transplant. That might explain all the well-dressed men coming in and out of here.

God knows, some or all of this may be true. Because I know for a fact that the numbering system for rooms on different floors doesn't add up; there are halls that lead nowhere, unsigned doors that are always locked, whole wards that are (unsecretly!) designated as secret, radiation signs in more places than there need to be, and the helicopter that lands on the seventh-floor pad doesn't always carry patients.

I know—everyone "knows"—that the fancy renovations of the well-known famous architect for the new medical center include plans for secret projects, secret rooms, some say a whole entire underground hospital.

And why shouldn't this be so? This is a great medical center, in a great university, in the third largest city (second largest city?) in the United States. It just seems strange, that's all. And then I hear two med students leaning against the wall behind me, snickering, saying, under their breath, "Did you hear about Shackleford boning that cooze in the bone-room, heh-heh?"

I wonder what my own son did, to provoke his wife to adultery. And I wonder when they say they've got some smallpox going on somewhere in here.

I don't like the look of that gate they've built behind me, although they say it's just for protection from gangs. But we don't have any gangs in Westwood, just that one shooting, years ago. So is it really, truly, a precaution for war? Is everybody on every side going to get it together and finally *declare* one?

Hard to know what to believe, one way or another.

I could go upstairs, to see him.

But I can't.

And I don't even have Melinda here to talk to. The Barclays don't come here at night.

Alone again! Alone *still*. I can't say I like that in any way at all.

PHIL

"You don't own this kitchen." Larry, belligerent.

Phil took a minute to think about it. "I *do* own this kitchen. Until the papers are final."

"You don't own the beer in the fridge."

"Come on, Larry. Don't be an asshole *all* your life." Phil put the beer down on the sink. *His* sink. "I'm just waiting for Vern, is all."

"You can wait for him in the car. I don't want Felicia to be any more upset."

Something about Larry made Phil yawn. He yawned expansively and—he couldn't help it—cracked open the beer, chugged half a can, swallowed hard. "Where is she, anyway? Usually she's got a lot of things to get off her chest."

"She needed me to talk to you today."

"Yeah? What about? We usually do our own talking."

"Felicia is very upset."

"You already said that."

It was true. Felicia was more upset than usual these days. During the first week or two, when they were still together but apart, she'd run through the house throwing herself on beds and couches and slamming doors and throwing cosmetics and pulling at her hair.

"Stingy! You're so stingy! My mother told me that about you!"

He'd felt himself redden. Had Janet really said that, the Janet he respected and loved? "I wasn't the one who fucked somebody else." His voice had risen to a nasty treble. "You always *were* going to fuck somebody else! *My* mother told me that about *you!*"

Which, of course, didn't help things and only persuaded Felicia that she'd been right in the first place to find somebody else.

Who'd moved into his house now, as far as Phil could tell, or at least was everywhere on the premises all the time.

"Do you only wear that one blue shirt?" Phil asked him suddenly. "I only ever see you wearing that blue shirt."

"I own several in this same color," Larry said. "Felicia has suggested that we talk. She says we need to talk."

"Go ahead." *In my kitchen.*

"As you know, it's been a difficult period of adjustment. For all of us."

"Yeah?"

"Felicia, especially, is . . ."

"Is *what*?"

"Eloise is doing as well as expected. As you know, we've placed her in therapy. She's responding well enough. She's her mother's child."

"I *know* it." Which came out sounding worse than he meant.

"Vernon is another matter entirely."

Something in Phil swelled. He crossed in front of the prick in the blue shirt to the refrigerator and pulled out another can of Tecate. Dared Larry to say something. Said, "He saw you two together. It messed with his disposition."

"Felicia tells me that Vernon's been this way for a *long* time: since he was born. A problem. A serious problem. An *untended* problem. And that you're very much a part of that problem."

"I'll take him," Phil said. "I'll take him right now, this afternoon, you bastard."

Larry smiled. "As I understand it, you're living in a hotel. You work long hours. You have no way of taking care of him. That was part of the problem in the first place, Felicia tells me; you were rarely around."

"She's a fucking liar!"

"That's enough."

But Phil outweighed this little jerk by forty pounds. He had right on his side besides. "She's a fucking *liar*!"

"She tells me that because of Vern's bad record this year, his only alternative this fall has been to enroll in a public middle school. I'm afraid I can't allow that. Not as the man who looks out for Felicia and her family's welfare."

There was such a thing as seeing red. It had to do with blood collecting in the retina. Or was it the optic nerve? "Give him to me," Phil muttered. "I'll take him with me today."

"You know that's out of the question. Felicia's children mean everything to her. Even you can't deny she's a wonderful mother. She's more than done her part. But Vernon is becoming a danger to himself and others."

"She's a liar," Phil said again. "I just didn't know it then—before."

"He has dangerous mood swings. He stays in the shower for hours at a time. He roars. He can scarcely speak the language, or doesn't choose to. He's broken the glass top on Felicia's dressing table; I suppose she told you about that. He's thrown her perfumes out the window. At dinner he refuses to talk. He points his fork at me in an unacceptable way. He's taken to wearing a stocking cap inside the house. He won't eat correctly. He's small for his age. He shuffles like a convict. He dresses like a gangster. His mother tells me he's given her the finger. His language is inexcusable."

"You said he didn't have any. Language."

"You're not getting the point. Felicia said you wouldn't. His behavior is unacceptable. Felicia and I have discussed this. I've been in touch with several out-of-state military schools. Really, they're the only option. He'll thank us for it later. Someone has to teach him the rudiments of good behavior—not to mention some basic academic skills. Frankly, that's not what I signed on for, here."

"Signed *on* for?" Phil's tongue was thick in his mouth.

"We'll try medications too. I'm sure Felicia has told you about that. But they won't solve the larger problem. The boy is frankly out of control. The tuition will be included in part of the settlement."

"Did you think this up?"

"Certainly. Certainly, I thought it up. But you can see—"

A noise on the back stairs. And there was Vern, his cap pulled down to his eyes, his pants hanging along his hips. His breathing was quick and shallow, his cheeks pale. He'd probably heard it all.

"There you go, Vern," his dad said. "Let's get going."

Larry wasn't finished. "Vernon has *excreted* on the couch. The living room couch. Is that enough for you?"

ANDREA

It had started this afternoon, their first terrible fight. Danny had said his mom was finally almost persuaded, and they were going to pull the plug on his uncle. She'd said she was sorry, but it hit him wrong some way, how she'd said it.

"But life is cheap with us," he said. "Everybody knows that."

"Did you love your uncle very much?" she asked, but he brushed that off too.

"People like us don't throw love around the way you do. We don't *drool* over it."

She hadn't known what to say, so she kept quiet. But as bad luck would have it, they were in the north campus cafeteria, eating out of rice-and-beef bowls with raw wooden chopsticks. He watched her sardonically, then said, "You couldn't do that around *my* house."

"What?"

"Around my house you'd have to wait. You'd have to learn some manners."

"You could learn a few yourself," she shot back, and immediately regretted it.

"The best woman on earth is lucky to be in the same room with the worst man." He looked at her, waiting for some kind of reply.

"What is that, some kind of fake proverb you made up? Isn't that kind of *cheap*?"

They'd gone on. She couldn't remember what they'd said, except she had asked him—in tears, "Where's the boy I knew in poetry class? Where did *that* go, Danny?"

And he'd gotten up and slammed off, without saying goodbye.

She was home now. They were sitting down to an early dinner, and she was feeling bruised and lost, when the phone rang. Her mom answered. "Yes, yes! . . . Yes, we'll be right over! We were just—is it all right if we have dinner? . . . Yes, all right. Of course . . . Thank you.

"That was someone on the staff down at the Medical Center. They want you to check in this evening; there's a kidney. They want to start your tests, in case it . . . works out."

Andrea felt sure her dad had known before her mother said a word. Because she'd known. She'd heard it with her mom's first *yes*.

The table they were sitting at was covered with a round lace tablecloth. Chicken and lemon, a green salad, a bowl of cranberry sauce because her dad liked it. Music playing: Brahms, something calm.

The phone call had come! A chandelier shed its yellow-colored light down on the three of them. Beyond them, shadowed, the piano, the books and quiet furniture, the French doors—closed against the chill—and then their patio.

"Well," her mother said. "We should eat something. Oh, God."

"It doesn't necessarily mean it's going to happen." Her father speaking now.

But they had never gotten so close.

They did eat; they managed. Andrea cleared the table, put the leftover chicken, wrapped in plastic, in the refrigerator. She stacked the dishes in the washer, wiped down the sink. Picked up a wall phone, called her closest girlfriend, whom she'd cried to, earlier, about Danny. "They think they might have a kidney for my dad . . . I know. I *know*! I'll call you later."

There was a mirror, a small one, over one of the counters. She checked her reflection. She looked wild and strange.

She went across the house into her parents' bedroom, where her mom was packing up a suitcase: pajamas, toothbrush, razor, slippers. Her moves were methodical but her hands trembled.

"Remember to take along some homework or a book," her mother said. "We don't know how long we'll be."

Andrea remembered the seminar the family had sat through with others on the waiting list, how if the kidney was a good match they could often do the operation almost immediately. Or if the donor was brain-dead, the family might still be reluctant to donate. Or if it was not a very good match they could still treat the blood to take out the antibodies and do the transplant anyway.

But none of this could be decided until it was decided.

Her dad was in his office, sorting through papers. He almost always had several projects going at a time. She watched his arms moving under his Brooks Brothers shirt, his hair falling over his eyes. "I need something harder than the Spanish," he said. "Something to keep my mind occupied. But not those Hungarians!"

He looked up and smiled at her, and she could see that he was afraid. Why did this have to happen to a man like him, a dear, kind, gentle man? Why did it have to happen to any of them?

He settled on some difficult poems in Catalan; it wasn't the language, he told her, but the thoughts, the precise diction, that was the challenge with them.

"This is good news," he said, "because even if tonight doesn't work out it means I'm way up on the list."

She nodded. And went to find something to read for herself.

Then they were driving the short mile or so down to the Med Center, past fraternity row, where crowds of kids in shorts walked in the night, some of them holding hands, most holding beers. Again, the lights out here were yellowish, golden. The kids glistened against the night.

They turned left, then left again, into the Med Center parking lot, then up and out across the big courtyard to Admissions, walking through that big familiar waiting room. Edith, at the desk, looked up and broke into a big smile, waved carefully at her mom.

She went with her parents to the various windows where you showed your hospital card, your faculty card, your driver's license, all that. Young interns, residents—so sure of themselves!—walked quickly by in twos and threes, talking about symptoms, impressing one another. The lights were bright. Families strolled by on their way to or from visits. There seemed to be a lot of extra people around.

They went up to the fourth floor, the three of them, to what would be his hospital room. Someone at the nurses' station said their doctor was on the way over.

Then everyone got shy.

"I'll just go and wait downstairs," Andrea said.

"You can come up later, when he's settled in," her mom said.

She went back down to the waiting room, past Edith, who said, "It's good news, isn't it." She thought about getting some tea from the cafeteria, decided against it, found a place on a couch, opened her book, then gave up and started listening and taking a look around.

A crowd of Latinos picked at a tray of something sugary and powdery. Exhausted white wives and husbands sat side by side. People who just had to be acquaintances of somebody were chatty and sociable, along for the ride, happy to be out and about, not stuck at home watching television. Another group she thought might be Persian maybe, burly and all dressed up with jewelry. After a while, she got it that they were taking turns going inside—up to intensive care, probably.

And, across the room, Danny's family, more of them than usual, his mother crying hard. Andrea recognized his two sisters from that awful day. One of them caught her eye and Andrea opened up her book, ignored her. She was fed up with them, with all that.

She actually read for a while, forgot where she was, reading Philip Roth, not thinking about anything but the story, when the main doors opened and maybe half a dozen Asian gangbangers trooped in, with low-slung Levi's and a ridiculous amount of chains and tattooed arms and sweatshirts with the sleeves cut off or white T-shirts rolled carefully up, so scowling, so dangerous-looking, she actually considered the thought that this might be part of some crime about to happen.

Danny came over to her. What had she been thinking, to get mixed up with him?

"What are you doing here?" he asked.

"They told my father there might be a kidney. If the tests go OK."

"My uncle's worse." He turned and swaggered away. The rest of them didn't even look at her.

The waiting room calmed down and people went back to what they were doing. She opened up her book again. The print didn't say anything.

As if he barely knew her.

She didn't have to take that. She was a beautiful blonde, and as kind as she was beautiful. And her father might be getting a kidney this very night. So she wouldn't take any meanness. Because she didn't have to. Because this was going to be over. She gave them all the haughtiest glance she could manage and went back to her story.

ANDREA

Of course, it took a couple of hours before anything happened at all. Andrea and her mother read and waited. They pulled out a deck of cards and played a few rounds of gin. Edith got up from her desk every once in a while and asked what she could do: Bring them coffee? Anything at all?

Around eleven at night a doctor came down, went over to Danny's family, got down on his haunches, and began to talk with some urgency, it seemed to her. It got to a place where he gestured across the room toward Andrea and her mom and a wail went up from the females. No, they were saying, no, it couldn't happen. Uncle Lao's organs weren't up for grabs, not by some round-eye! Or that's what Andrea thought.

She wasn't a girl to lose her temper but she got up, crossed the room, stood in front of May—the one who couldn't or wouldn't speak English. "You know," she said, "you don't have to be rude. There's no point to it. None of this is our fault. *You* don't have the right to be rude to me. I was a guest in your house. Don't you people have any manners?" Then, to Danny, "I made a big mistake! You're just a bully. All the poetry in the world can't cover that up."

They stared at her.

"Well," she said, "that's what I wanted to say." The tears started and she brushed them away. "*My* dad is dying. Will anything bring your uncle back? No."

She walked back across the room. The doctor, who'd stood like a statue while she talked, got down on his haunches again, went on talking.

"It might not work out," Andrea said to her mom. "I guess you know that."

Edith, who'd come by again, shook her head. "I hate to see this," she said.

But then she looked past Andrea to the big front doors. "What is it?" Edith said. "What's wrong?"

Her son, Dr. Fuchs, who Andrea recognized, had even been introduced to once or twice, grabbed his mother's arm. "I have to talk to you, right now."

"What is it?"

"I've got Vern outside in the car. . . ."

And that was the last Andrea could hear clearly after that, except, "You've got to help me!"

Edith was at her desk now. Her son had pulled up a chair and taken both her hands. "I don't *know*!" Andrea heard. "I don't know what I *can* do. He can't come to my house—that would be the first place they'd look. Oh, I always hated that woman! She *would* pull something like this."

Then, from across the room, the doctor moved toward them. Andrea and her mother waited. Her mother trembled. No one, Andrea thought, should have to go through what my mom is going through.

"The Lee family has decided," the doctor said, "to give you a kidney."

His voice rang out and Edith's son heard. He laughed and put his head in his hands. "I'm not giving up. I won't. I can't," he said to his mother.

Then he did a strange thing. He swiveled his chair so that it faced the waiting room, leaned way back, straightened his legs, locked his hands behind his head.

"What next?" he said.

"Andrea, dear, I'm going upstairs to see your dad. I want to be the one to tell him." But first her mother went across to Danny's mom, knelt, and thanked her.

Danny came over to Andrea. "I'm in way over my head with you, you must know that. What I said this afternoon—some of that was really true. When you sit down to a family dinner at my house, you have to wait a little for the guys to eat, or you'll catch hell for it. It's the way we do things. But don't you think this is hard for me too, hard for all of us? Trying to figure out how to live over here? I don't care, Andrea. I've got to have you, I think, any way I can."

Andrea listened, but other things were happening in here. They distracted her. Along the wall of the room, a guy was hastily laying some wire along the floor. A couple of workmen appeared behind Edith and her son, checking the new metal lattice gate they'd been working on for the last month or so. Andrea could hear a helicopter buzzing. Of course they always had helicopters around here, but still—

A low whining started, four short beeps and a long one. Dr. Fuchs got up and listened for a minute or two. He laughed again.

"Absolutely not!" he said. "No way!" He wrenched his mother from her chair and called out across the room, "Time to get out, people! We're having a little drill here, is all. Let's go. Let's *go*!"

"I should wait," Andrea said. "I can't go without my mom." But the doctor had hold of her now. And the lattice was clanking shut.

"Come on!" Phil rounded up the others. "Look sharp. It's just a drill, but you don't want any part of it!"

Then they were all out on the wide front steps, hesitating, wondering what to do, where to go, what next. Danny's family chattered. There was an element of excitement to it all, in spite of poor Uncle Lao.

"Can we go somewhere and talk?" Danny asked Andrea. "Figure out a way to make it right?"

She nodded. It seemed to her that something really big had happened, not just to her or to her mother and father. The past had been cut off somehow and they were already living in the future, all of them.

What will it mean to me? she thought, as they walked slowly

down the wide brick courtyard and the insistent whine faded behind them. Will I really give my life to this boy? She thought of life, how mysterious and strange it was, how different it was for every single human being.

When they went down into the parking lot, she saw them again, Edith and her son, leaning against what must be his car, still talking. She could see, dark against the glow of the artificial lights, the head of a small boy, all alone.

PHIL

Phil had a satchel full of money; fifties, hundreds. All the papers he might need. Passports. And two other pieces of luggage, duffel bags lumpy with his possessions. His doctor's black bag lay on the passenger seat of the car, where it could be seen by anyone who stopped to check, and many did. He wore his laminated identification card around his neck. And he had his honest, worried face.

The harbor was darker than he would have thought, dim lights flicking blue from under warehouse roofs. He stopped and drank some coffee in the car, just down from the Vincent Thomas Bridge. Walls of black slid past, the huge sides of ships stacked with crates. He could hear hushed human voices from the decks, hidden from his view. Boys in uniform stuck their heads in the car every few minutes. They too kept their voices low. Philip wasn't afraid. "I'm waiting for a call," he said importantly, pointing to his ID. "I'm waiting for a call." And they left him alone.

He drove around slowly to get his bearings; he had all the rest of the night to find it. Around midnight he spotted one of the bedraggled freighters he'd been looking for, loading up. A lonely crane deposited goods. In a kiosk at the land end of a fairly short gangplank, a middle-aged man did paperwork under dim light. Philip got out of the car and went over, carrying his bags.

"Where you going?"

The man looked up, over bent reading glasses. Didn't bother to answer.

"They need a doctor? Where're they headed?" For perhaps the tenth time that night, he indicated his identification. He zipped open his black bag, the one his stepfather, terribly proud, had given him when he got his MD. Extra prescription drugs in there. Extra potassium. Extra syringes. Antibiotics. Sedatives.

God, it was damp. A hot, hot night. Corrosive, salty. He breathed carefully against the constriction in his chest. Everything in him wanted to cough. He could hear the water a few feet away, a few feet below, just being water. A thin sound.

"San Diego, Veracruz, Galveston, Marseille, Stockholm, Oslo, Suez, and down through the Indian Ocean, subject to change from the world situation."

A scrape up on deck caught their attention. Someone swore— or it sounded like it—in a foreign language.

"Could I talk to the captain?"

"He's Portuguese. You could try to talk to him."

"I've got some French. And some Spanish."

The guy in the kiosk stared out. Something else had his attention. Another ship loomed up and went by.

"So, is it true they closed the hospitals up in LA?"

Philip shrugged. "Probably just a drill." Remembering the girls with the split fingers and the fevers, and the security guy in the Palomino, and the siren, sounding so tentative and wimpy, after all, four shorts and one long. Remembering how a ship like this had sailed north from Manzanillo, maybe on a night like this, to the port of Los Angeles, and a cab had taken a couple from the ship in the year 1926, all the way downtown.

"Have you ever shipped out?"

Phil didn't think it was worth an answer. He listened to the water. Watched the guy place a call.

"Crew of fifteen. If things go wrong they'll want a doctor. Some speak English. You'll get a cabin. Got a passport?"

Phil reached in his inside coat pocket, reached in, flicked it open. An open-faced fool looked out at them both.

"What'll you do with the car?" pointing with his chin.

"Leave it. Someone will pick it up."

"Need help with your bags?"

"I'll carry them."

Just like that, then. Walking up a gangplank, steep and narrow, not like the cruise ships he'd been on, but there were narrow crossbars to help your footing. He gasped, going up, his duffel bags heavy on his shoulders. Then on deck, standing on glistening, dripping metal. Shaking hands with a squat man. Shaking hands with another. Placing his bags carefully on the deck and as carefully picking them up. Being led into a cabin, unused, two bunks, seeing that, thank God, there was nobody else in here. Thinking this ship must have been one of the last freighters from the old days, with room for a few passengers.

Who knew when it would sail? Who knew when the quarantine would start, or if it would? Who knew about possible blockades, at ports, at state lines, at border towns?

He reached into one of his bags. Six quarts of vodka, right near the top, wrapped in underwear and clean scrubs. He opened a bottle, drank from it. All they had to do was make a call, to turn him in. Some kind of fugitive. On the other hand, he was a doctor. A better one than they'd ever see again.

He heard steps outside the door. He was too tired to think about it. They'd have to do what they needed to do. Just as he'd done what he needed to do. He found a lock on the door, tried to make it work. Maybe it did. The light in here glared. The walls, green metal. A basin with a rust stain. A toilet, with a shower right above it. No towels. But the bunks had blankets, sheets. He straightened up, turned down the covers of both bunks.

Philip stooped over the heavier duffel bag, pulled out bunched-up T-shirts, sweats, extracted a pale, bare scrawny leg, then another. Heaving, pushing, gasping, he shucked the bag off of Vernon, the kid breathing OK but out like a light. Philip turned down the sheets on the bottom bunk and, grunting with exertion, the end of all his effort, tumbled his son in.

Who cared? No one. Who was going to care? He was prepared to stay in this room for days, weeks, until they shipped out, ready to keep Vernon doped up forever if he had to. But near dawn he

heard a series of clanks, metal upon metal, voices in different languages, a grinding noise far away, and then a sensation of moving.

He lay in the top bunk, right on the edge, his hand dangling
down to Vern, who slept silently and soundly. The ship moved
and moved, seemed to stop, then after half an hour moved again,
began to heave lightly. Philip rolled over, rummaged in his bag,
slapped seasick patches on them both.

Someone pounded at the metal door. Phil opened it to find a
swarthy steward with a cup of tea. He eyed the boy in the bunk
and came back with another cup. "Breakfast, twenty minutes,"
he said.

Phil went to shake his son awake and found him with his eyes
open and wary.

"For God's sake, keep your mouth shut," he told Vern. "Don't
say anything until I give you the go-ahead. I mean it."

They used the toilet, washed their faces. Phil combed his son's
hair, jerking hard.

Was this a hall, or did they have a nautical word for it? The
steward (if that's what he was) gestured down the hall (if that's
what it was) and toward a room with bright lights, a table, and
about a dozen men.

"Dr. Fuchs," he said. "I'm Dr. Philip Fuchs, and this is my
son, Vernon."

The men looked up but didn't stop eating.

"Igor."

"Vasili."

"Domingo."

"Dareholt. Victor Dareholt."

"Fong Cheun."

"Fong Yuen."

"Roy Farthington."

And the others.

Victor told them to sit down. The captain was up on deck.
Oatmeal appeared before them. "Bring the boy a glass of milk,"
Victor said. "This the first time you've shipped out, son?"

Vernon looked at his dad. Philip nodded.

"Yes, sir."

The man nodded. Philip locked his eyes on Vern, who put a
napkin in his lap, held it there with his left hand, put out his
right, and took a cautious sip of milk.

Conversation began again, low, weary, in different languages.
Victor looked at Phil. "How about you?"

"What?"

"First time shipping out? Got your papers?"

"Yes. No. I teach and practice at UCLA."

Victor nodded, shrugged. And that was that.

2007–2016

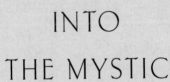

INTO
THE MYSTIC

PHIL and VERNON

It was how he'd imagined it, if he'd had time to imagine it. San
Diego—in a matter of hours after the first scare—had closed to
shipping. They sailed on past. They went through the Panama
Canal, nobody on, nobody off. They had a day's shore leave in
Veracruz, a day of clouds and rain, when he and Vernon listened
to marimba players in the downtown square and then took a cab
to a thatched-roof restaurant on the shore, where Phil ordered a
green coconut with rum in it and Vern drank an Orange Crush.

"Dad," Vern said. "Check out the crabs."

He did. He checked out the crabs, big as dinner plates, chugging out across the gray sodden sand from the sea to the highway,
chugging on back. He also checked out the sound of his son's

voice, a strange, light, and sandy-seeming tenor, dizzy with—could it be happiness? Ordered another round for both of them and some fish tacos.

Like what he had imagined but not what he imagined. Spending the days, those first few weeks, from ten in the morning to one in the afternoon, seeing any of the crew who stopped by, big guys or small, with weathered faces, tattooed or not, guys who needed aspirin for flu or wrappings for torn ligaments or casts for broken bones. There was a good supply of antibiotics on board and a jury-rigged doctor's office with glassed-in cupboards. Remedies from other countries lined the shelves as well—guys who had little English reached or pointed to what they wanted, mimed what he was supposed to do: rub it on them, offer it to them to swallow.

He'd imagined—if he did imagine—that sex and drugs would be a problem on board a ship, for Vernon or for him. But homemade alcohol and crashing hangovers and a few joints seemed to describe the extent of the crew's vices; he gave them aspirin, salt tablets, told them to drink tomato juice. If the sailors buggered each other, he didn't know about it or want to know.

In just the first few weeks—and then the months—he watched his kid turn back into a good kid. Heard him, with his mates, laughing. Watched him wash windows or swab the deck. Or hang out with Cheun or Vasili or Domingo, trying to learn their languages. Watched him in the long evenings, playing chess or checkers or letting a guy teach him to read—again, in some whole other language.

They worked the kid pretty hard. Taught him to cook. He racked up wages. Got strong and tan. Phil made a pact with himself to lay off any "dad talks," never to improve him, not "explain" anything unless he was asked.

Driving back in a cab to the dock in hot, dank gray rain, that first afternoon in Veracruz, they stopped off at a store for cigarettes, soap, newspapers.

"USA once more at the brink," Vern translated. He did have a terrific gift for languages.

Still, the epidemic, as such, seemed to have petered out. This paper, at least, suggested it could have been more propaganda than reality. Another false alarm. (Or not.)

Phil said, "You want another Orange Crush for the ship?"

"Sure."

Maybe a week into their voyage, as they slipped through Mexican waters, Vern asked casually, "Does Mom know what we're doing?"

"I e-mailed her. She's pissed, but she's all right. Don't worry, Vern. She's being taken care of."

Vern grinned.

And just like that, Phil finessed the whole crying, blaming, weeping, dish-throwing extended drama about divorce, remarriage, military school, and that possibly upcoming baby brother (or sister, as the case might be).

But didn't he feel bad? Didn't he feel lost? Didn't he worry about lost opportunities? Lost family? Lost home? No sex? No wife? No daughter? No tennis? No ground to walk on? No. No. No. No. No. No. No. No. Except for his mother, he didn't miss any of it. He did miss her, though. Worried about her.

Back from that first day on shore, Phil walked up the gangplank in his hooded anorak, watching Vern's anorak in front of him. It could have been the rum, but his muscles, even his bones, felt loose and clean and free.

Galveston wouldn't let them dock. The on-again off-again scare. Fifty-seven deaths in that city, and counting. They sailed past Miami and out into the Atlantic, headed to Oslo, then Stockholm, then Dover. The captain huddled in his office making arrangements, changing plans. (But there was no trouble about essential supplies. Tenders, even in the American ports, had come out with water and staples.) Imports in America were at a standstill during the pending situation. But what was the hurry? Millions of dollars may have hung in the balance as profit or loss, but they weren't his millions.

Of course, there was e-mail and ship-to-shore radio and phones and TV, but the crew didn't take much advantage of these conveniences. They hung out, kidded Vernon, showed their usually harmless symptoms to Phil. The general feeling on the ship was: If they'd wanted to keep up with things on land, they would have stayed on land.

Something about Oslo's pristine cleanliness during their second stop made Phil call his wife. He didn't kid himself about how she'd receive him, what she'd do when she picked up the phone. They'd exchanged furious e-mails, but she had control of his bank account and investments. She had her plans.

Still, hearing her voice, he had an unsettling vision of what he'd left behind: his den, his cave of wine under the staircase, his Dutch door. The tennis courts on the campus at UCLA. The ratty lawn by the pool at the Rec Center with pale assistant professors and their fretful children. The air in LA that never cleared up but always surprised him with its weird beauty. His daughter and her practiced sneers. His wife. His responsibilities, abdicated. He'd run out on them all.

Felicia surprised him. Her first words: "Are you all right?"

"Yes. I'm fine. I'm in Oslo. It's raining. What about you?"

"Is Vernon OK?"

"He is. Just listen, Felicia. Listen to this. You'll like this." And he told her about a night just a week or so out when Vern, a little bored, began to act up at dinner. He'd tried it twice, that trick of his, slamming the table with the flat of his hand. The first time Phil had said, "Vern!" The second time, Vasili had grabbed the kid's arm, bent back his hand, and growled, *"Nyet!"* And Vern stopped. Didn't say a word or do anything the whole rest of the meal. "He's gone back to reading again. He's been playing chess. And he's beginning to pick up some Russian and Spanish and even Chinese. So . . . I don't know. Maybe I did the wrong thing —"

She sighed. "I'm getting married as soon as the divorce comes through. And the baby is coming. Except it's twins."

"That's good, Felicia."

"It's all right. Larry goes along with me. You never did go along with me. You stayed in your own world. I got so lonely!"

"I know. I'm sorry."

"When Larry and I go into places? His friends always say hello to me. He loves to cook. And he really likes Eloise. We're beginning to entertain. We go to the tennis club for brunch. After the babies, I'm going to start taking lessons. I should have done that with you."

He thought of the closed wards at UCLA. The mysterious new diseases. His chest caught at the precariousness of it. All of it.

"What if things get iffy again? In the country?"

"Remember, Larry's in security. He says he'll know when to get us out. He says you went off half cocked." Then she giggled, a sound he hadn't heard in years.

"Do you get on his case about the blueberries from Ralph's instead of Gelson's, the way you did with me?"

"He always gets the right kind, Phil."

"Listen, Felicia. This harbor is beautiful. I don't know what I like best, the hot places like Veracruz or Tampico or the cold places, the way it is here. Lots of times we don't even get off the ship, we don't really know for sure where we are, but it's beautiful, more beautiful than I ever thought, more beautiful than I could have ever imagined. God, Fel . . ."

And he talked, went on talking, until gently, she told him she had to get off the phone. "But I'm glad you called. I'm really glad."

"Me too."

"And are you in touch with your mother?"

"Yes. Mostly by e-mail."

"She still keeps on at the Med Center, even though you're gone. I'd like to do something for her, but I don't know what."

"Just put up with her, if you can. Send her an announcement when those kids get born."

"Phil? If it wasn't for the emergency, or Larry and Vern, would you have—? It's none of my business, I know I did an awful thing to you."

He couldn't answer. It had been for Vern, what he'd done. But he was so glad he had done it.

"Will you call me again? Will you tell Vern I love him?"

"Sure. I'll call so much Larry will get jealous."

She laughed. "He already *is*! He *loves* me! He hates to have me out of his sight."

EDITH

In the year after Phil took Vern away, I learned some more about loneliness. My son wouldn't leave my thoughts. I sat at that desk in the waiting room and waited. Every time the door opened to a man in a white starched coat, I saw him. Then I thought, No, he's just gone in the side door today. Then I remembered. And I remembered my grandson. How could I have been so thoughtless, so selfish? How could I have let that boy slip through my fingers? How could I have heard about the trouble he was getting in and not done something—anything—about it?

Two words I got used to in that year. *Lost. Gone.* Hamilton was gone and lost to me—his academic niceties, the way he presumed to teach me "taste." As if, Hamilton, taste meant anything at all! And Charlie. I kept his suede jacket so I could put my face in it, but during that year the jacket turned into something on a hanger, nothing more. Because Charlie was gone. And my son— I knew—wasn't coming back. He e-mailed me sometimes, and Vern did too, sometimes. But he stopped calling because I cried when he did. My son was lost to me! Lost and gone.

Then, somewhere around my seventieth birthday, walking the floor alone pretty late at night, drinking vodka, crying, I heard myself saying out loud, pretty dramatically, "I'm drowning, I'm drowning!" Then I thought, Well, nothing you can do can change it. And I thought, What if I live underwater for a change, see what's down there? Take what little cash I have and let the credit go. *Really* keep my eyes open this time! And I've tried to do that. Because, really, what else is there to do when something's lost and gone? Let it go. Let it drift away.

Last Saturday, I had lunch with my women's group.

The way it goes is: We have lunch at one woman's house. Each of us brings a dish. We talk, we laugh, we exchange pleasantries, we sit down. Then we each take a turn, talking about our lives, what we've been doing in the past month, whether things are going well for us or not.

Our lunches include chicken livers, sautéed in a secret way. Many salads, most often with home-grown ingredients, peppers, tomatoes, mangoes, avocados, walnuts, pine nuts. Fresh corn, grilled, with more fresh tomatoes.

We talk about ourselves. We can't help it. Of course, the

country is hopeless. Our own lives are what we're stuck with. They're fairly interesting lives. One wife went off with her husband, who was directing a movie in the middle of Africa, and came back with the news: They hate us. They don't just dislike Americans, they *hate* us! She wasn't allowed off the compound and into the city. She wasn't even allowed to walk *around* the compound without a couple of African bodyguards. Because if the natives had caught her alone they would have killed her. She said.

She's a nice woman! So are we all! The salads come together on our plates, the marvelous dressings pooling underneath the greens. The respected playwright, the fountain designer, the lady who's working with the ashes of the dead to make miniature monuments—art objects—to display on the necks of the bereaved, the desks of the bereaved, all of them show up. We're widows, mostly.

We talk about how we used to dread our husbands' deaths, of how we'd hear a thud in the other room, and how our husbands might call out ironically, anticipating our worry, "It's just a book. I only dropped a *book*." I mention that very nice man I stopped going out with because I couldn't stand the suspense. We talk about how some of the poor guys wore out their welcome. We talk about brave men on walkers or in wheelchairs, keeling over on social occasions in freshly pressed khakis, passing out prone on green, well-watered lawns. In public places. And we were supposed to do something about it.

We have enough money, generally speaking, to eat out in good restaurants. (Or we may not, but we do anyway.) We make some of the best conversation in the world. We're funny and well informed. We include fine artists and a wonderful woman who makes documentary films in Middle Eastern outposts like Tajikistan. We know more about the world than many.

And, as I know I've said before, we're of no importance whatsoever. We are only one of the choruses. Only an audience. We deplore the blood-crazed leaders of the world. We watch them on television. We demonstrate against wars. But in the truest sense, we can't get arrested.

Of what use are we in society? (We talk about that.) Strictly speaking, not much. We don't take care of children very much, anymore. We are cut off—or have cut ourselves off—from the society of couples. We tend, or tended, our dying or dead husbands. We loved them and miss them. Some things aren't often said. "I romanticize David so much in my memory," Joyce said last week, "I almost don't remember anymore how he used to complain."

"Complain!" Margie chimed in. "Every time Daylight Savings Time came around, I'd hear about it for a week at least."

"Douglas always hated Standard Time. The wastefulness of it."

"Egg-white omelets. Paul demanded egg-white omelets."

And I'd be forced to remember an old boyfriend of mine who whirred raw liver in a blender, slugged it down for breakfast, and followed me around, grinning with pink teeth.

And then they expect you to have sex with them.

But they are sweet.

And they do give you kids.

But then, how much fun are the kids? (When you're honest about it.)

Sometimes, one of us will cry. We *are* alone. Some of us are still putting children through school. Or driving to work. Many of us were passed over for promotions. Or not even passed over, simply ignored. I've cried there for my son, whom I can't see anymore. My grandson.

We have cancer worries. Some of us are already cancer survivors. Another gives a series of university seminars in which she assigns papers that ask, "If none of you had ever seen a fork before, how would you design a fork?"

One possible use we have in our society is that we know a fair amount about it and have come to be against it in almost every way. We sneer at the Secretary of Defense, for instance, and make fun of his hypothetical performances in bed. (But one of us, whose cousin works in Washington, says, "It isn't funny, really. That guy is a piece of work. Especially with women.") And we let the subject drop.

But it stays there, in our collective conversation. And we might pass it on.

And then we talk about why so many women of every age (still) play dumb, and men feel called upon to play smart.

We are as invisible as our mothers' glass curtains, porous as sieves. But if there are enough of us, maybe, hanging out in courtyards in Lebanon, playing canasta in Mazatlán on a winter afternoon, sharing cuttings and home-grown avocados on a backyard California lawn, maybe—like those nuns rumored to be somewhere praying 24/7 for peace—maybe, possibly, we calm down the rage of men, the way the hardworking whores outside Las Vegas can fuck the meanest wildest truck drivers into decent behavior for a couple of hours or so.

And then I think of my darling second husband, who didn't have a murderous bone in his whole sweet body. If anything, I was the murderous one. And maybe the little use I have been was just to raise my son, who's happy now.

Or maybe I'm of no use at all. I imagine that might be the general consensus.

And sometimes I drop by to see Melinda and John, just to see how they're doing, and help myself to her delicious cookies, which she makes with so much love that some of it spills over into me.

EDITH

DEAR PHIL,

Things are much the same here, either tense or peaceful or both. But last Saturday I went over to the mainland for the weekend. I had dinner with friends and then, on Sunday, drove to Pasadena for a christening—of Danny and Andrea's third baby. Do you remember them? She's Melinda Barclay's daughter.

He's done very, very well; he works as an investment officer at Cathay Bank. She's decided, for a while at least, to stay home with the kids. And Pasadena has a large, worldly Asian community—the Pacific Asia Museum is there, and one of the oldest "Oriental" art stores in America. They live in a nice Craftsman on the edge of the arroyo, above the Rose Bowl, close to what used to be called Suicide Bridge. I suppose it's because of my age that I get a kick out of seeing flocks of Chinese and other "miscellaneous" people in what used to be such a bastion of stuffy white respectability. Of course, what is respectability anymore, and what was it ever?

At the christening, I walked down the driveway to the backyard, a half acre of lawn with those round rented tables, big oak trees draped with streamers and dragon banners. The place was wild with little kids; Sally is five, Lynette is three, and they had plenty of friends and plenty of anxious mothers following them around, trying to keep them from killing each other.

They're at that interesting age, Danny and Andrea, where, when all else fails, you have to become an adult or shut up about the whole thing. (Not an age I look back on with any nostalgia at all!) Danny has gained about forty pounds and it looks strange on him. But he's plainly happy. This new little boy, Tyrus—named after a famous California-Chinese artist—obviously delights him. And he was surrounded by people I've never really seen before, or really looked at— dozens and dozens of prosperous Chinese businessmen, slapping one another on the back and exchanging business cards, while their wives, slim and beautiful Chinese women, looked faintly as if they'd rather be anywhere else than on this hot and crowded lawn. And there were about 50 percent whites, also sweating and harried, also running after their toddlers.

Andrea looked exhausted, as well she might. Three kids!

And this huge party! She looks her age and more so. But that's . . . just the way it is. The three- and five-year-olds are hellions. Sally stole some potato chips off another kid's plate, that kid burst into tears, his friend pushed Sally and she socked him, the chips fell to the ground, other mothers rushed in, and so on.

Melinda and John, whom I got to know very well when he was in the hospital waiting for his transplant, seemed very chipper. She did the amiable hostess thing, going around from table to table. Her husband is translating another novel (of course). This one's Gypsy, the language is "Rroma." I thought of you and Vern.

Danny has grown rather fond of the sound of his voice. (Or am I just tired of listening to people?) He had plenty to say about finally having a son.

And of course he's done very well. I wonder if it had anything to do with his former gang ties? I remember so well that time when he and his family and all those "dangerous" boys with tattoos filled up the lobby. All I can say is, there had to be money there.

Oh, Phil! This really isn't sounding like the cheerful letter I wanted it to be. But I have to admit I came away a little sad—maybe it was envy or loneliness, but I don't think so. I was sad for them, maybe all of them. The whole thing (and what do I mean by *that*?) takes so much work, so much to-ing and fro-ing and running around on the lawn and wiping away tears.

I do know one thing, though. Nobody was worried about the ongoing or upcoming war. And I did think, driving home—or back to the harbor before I got the Catalina boat—that the thing about children is, they push away any other world. Until someone literally drops a bomb on the Rose Bowl, I don't think Andrea or Danny will think a thing about war, or anything else.

And they're just one couple. How about the Russians and the Armenians and, God knows, the Hispanics? They're all having parties for their kids out on some lawn or other and they don't have the time to watch television or wonder, when they sneeze, if this is the beginning of the end. So I guess that's another way to deal with it.

I told Andrea I was still in touch with you, but to be honest I don't think she remembers exactly who you are. "He was around for your father's transplant," I told her, but the poor woman was about to drop. She was holding the baby and trying to smile and guests were leaving and I think the girl she'd hired as a baby-sitter was off talking on a cell phone. Her own girls were screaming like banshees, throwing paper plates of ice cream. No one likes to have attention taken away by a baby brother.

And I thought, She didn't have to go to war to be conquered. Then I thought, *It's what happens!* You grow up, you have kids, you get old, and then you die. No big deal. (Unless you get lucky, and something interesting comes up.)

Now I'm back safe and sound, "twenty-six miles across the sea." Taking bridge lessons and collecting Catalina pottery, did I tell you? It's too expensive to buy here but I spend an hour or two on eBay every day. The buying is fun, the bargain-hunting is fun, and it's a great way to be sociable and chat with people from all over without getting messy about it. I love that pottery, Phil! I love the bright colors. I love it that the dishes are so sturdy and the vases are so strange and weird, actually. Humans are *weird,* right down to their cups and saucers. (Andrea may be the happiest woman in the world, for all I know.)

Take care, dear. And keep me apprised of everything you do.

xxx
Mom

PHIL

TO: Edith@earthlink.net
July 15, 2016

DEAR MOM,

"OK, fold me the fancy napkin, please." That's what the Bulgarian bartender asked him to do, and I guess that started it. Vern's on a cruise ship now, as you know.

He's doing very well. He started cleaning staterooms and then working the night shift for room service, and now he's a bartender in the ship's best bar. It was his gift for languages that got him promoted. There are people on board from everywhere—passengers and crew—Bulgaria, South Africa, America, France, Spain, Macedonia. And Arab countries too.

I took part of a cruise with him, through the Mediterranean. My first vacation in years. Vern was Mr. Suave. Lots of self-important customers—"Johnnie Walker Black on the rocks, *please*!" And jerk-offs coming up to the bar—"Can I have a glass of cold water?"—without even remembering to say please. Vern doesn't care. (Did he ever say *please* in his life? Except maybe to get laid. Which I don't want to know about.)

He's so tall now. His ship is a small one, taken over from the old Renaissance line, and the talk of the crew now is, "It's not the Renaissance!" If you ask them what that means, they pretend not to know what you're talking about. It's that language thing. They can always be Bulgarian if they have to be. And can I tell you about my stewardess? She's tall and blond and beautiful and Polish with a last name that's spelled Czrewsklwe, something like that. I did what I could to charm her but struck out—this time. I hope I didn't embarrass Vern.

One night he took me down to see the rest of the crew's quarters. It's like the rooms he grew up in with me, only bigger and much more crowded. I felt like I did when I was his dad in the old days: *Can't you kids pick up anything?* Because while my stateroom was—you know—clean and spacious, here were all those kids with wet towels on the floor, and unmade bunks, and girls crying away, and boys teasing them. I envied him, Ma. I got married before I had much fun. I think you did too. We didn't get the chance.

Another afternoon in the bar (and I felt strange being my son's guest, he looked so good, but he was *Vern*, you know?) a red airplane flew right in front of that big window with the spectacular view of the wake. I did everything to escape it, but you can't escape it, I thought. Here it is. But the plane flew by.

I'm back on the *Andorra* now. It's just the same as it ever was. I guess I'm getting too old for it, but I wouldn't be anywhere else. We're a bunch of old guys. Some of us have stayed with the ship for years. They can't get to you out here. You know what I mean? When we tie up in a place and are allowed ashore, I go to town for good wine. They kid me about it, but what are you going to do? I'm in charge of medications and nothing else. I watch the world go by. We came out of Amsterdam yesterday afternoon. It takes about three hours to hit the open sea and we pass house after house, boat after boat. Then plenty of green grass and maybe a concrete abutment. And maybe one guy out there, watching the traffic. And that's it. I hardly ever have to step on land again, if I don't want to. And I don't want to.

They tease me about you sometimes. They say I've got a soul mate. I say, well, what if I do? These conversations mean a lot to me.

Love,
Phil

EDITH

They went on, then, father and son, through calm and stormy seas. I keep in touch, or Phil keeps in touch, e-mailing or calling from everywhere without regard for time zone. He was never a master of light conversation, and he's gotten stranger over the years. "What are you drinking?" he'll ask. "What are you having for dinner tonight? Going out? Are you going out with anybody good? Or just the girls?" And, once, surprisingly: "I always thought of you as kind of a glamour girl. For your age, I mean."

I only laughed.

It's been fifteen years since Charlie died. The "real war" hasn't happened yet. Many little ones have. Epidemics and chemicals and explosives have ravaged certain parts of the globe—the trick,

I suppose, is to stay off the beaten track, whatever the track may be. The talk is mostly about China now. The "yellow menace" all over again.

Vernon lives the high life. He's still working on that cruise ship, master of several languages, darkly handsome, more than available to dance with lonely women. His life is pleasure, or the pursuit of it. To his father's amusement, he's a connoisseur of fine—and awful—wines. Vern hasn't once seen his mother since he left. Again—I hear this in rushed and sometimes drunken monologues from his father—he knew from the beginning who loved him and who did not. Vern e-mails me now and again, so I guess I sneaked in under the wire.

I never see Eloise and can't say I miss the experience.

Except for my monthly women's group, I don't stay on the mainland anymore. Like Phil, like Vern, I headed out. I took the hydrofoil into the Pacific twenty-six miles out to Catalina. It was and is another world. The town of Avalon, only ten blocks in each direction, streets of California bungalows bordered by trimmed trees of deadly nightshade. On summer days it teems with tourists, but the winters are soft and dreamy. I've joined a dance club that meets at the old casino on the bay. The ceilings there are dotted with fake stars, the polished floor takes us, swirling, into a world we never really knew in life. The old men are dapper beyond belief, the old women beautiful.

Not Dead Yet is the category by which we describe ourselves. That phrase covers a lot of ground. In fairness, you can say the warriors who live in all those warring countries on both sides, on every side, are "not dead yet." The demonstrating thousands in whatever arid Arab land are not dead yet. The politicians are not dead yet. Nor are Felicia and her offspring. The viruses, the poisons, the chemicals, the "dirty" bombs, the bacteria are certainly not dead yet.

But where I live, people ride bikes and tiny runabout golf carts. They grow zinnias and morning glories. The high school baseball games are well attended. The bars at night and the churches in the morning are always full.

Sure, there is terror and war somewhere, and sure, we all will die. But we're not dead yet! The enigmatic Vernon—I've seen the pictures his loving father sends—approaches sweet plump matrons each night and glides them out onto a tilting floor. His father makes his weekly phone calls to women he has loved and liked (he seems to have girls in every port), pouring out the story of his strange and very beautiful heart. And every weekend night I walk down the salty, dewy avenues past Catalina's tiny waterfront, out to the brightly lit casino.

We dance, mostly to rhythms from sixty, seventy, eighty years ago. We wish everyone well, but we don't want to be bothered. We've served our time, been duly terrorized, by death and bad stories of every kind. We're past that now.

We dance. We dance.

Thanks to:

LISA SEE

CLARA STURAK

LINDA KAMBERG DE MARTINEZ

LEE BOUDREAUX

NANCY MILLER

LEA BERESFORD

ADELAIDE DOCX

JANET H. BAKER

and

WARNE AND LEE

THERE WILL NEVER BE ANOTHER YOU

⁓

CAROLYN SEE

A Reader's Guide

A Conversation with Carolyn and Lisa See

Lisa See is Carolyn See's daughter. She is the author of five novels, including the recent Peony in Love, *the critically acclaimed* New York Times *bestseller* Snow Flower and the Secret Fan, Flower Net *(which was nominated for an Edgar Award),* The Interior, *and* Dragon Bones. *She is also the author of the widely acclaimed memoir* On Gold Mountain. *She lives in Los Angeles.*

Lisa See: I was excited and honored when Random House asked me to do this Q & A with you. You're my mom, and you've been a huge inspiration to me. I suppose I also know more about you and your writing life than anyone else on the planet. Even so, there are plenty of things I don't know, and this gives me the chance to ask those questions.

Carolyn See: Sweetest Lisa, it's just a joy to be having this conversation with you. It's true, you probably know more about me as a writer than anyone else in the world. And I take credit that I think I was the first one to recognize the tremendous literary importance of *Snow Flower and the Secret Fan.* I think it compares to Andre Malraux's *Man's Fate,* and said so from the first. It's so cool that we can talk to each other as writers.

L.S.: You've written a lot about the mother-daughter relationship, but in *There Will Never Be Another You,* you've focused on the father-son relationship. Why did you do that, and was it more difficult to write?

C.S.: In *Another You,* I write about fathers and sons because mothers have a tendency to annex child rearing for themselves, as in "You make the money, I'll take care of the kids." But when men have children they're looking at heritage, legacy, a shot at immortality. Phil, in *Another You,* has had not one but two fathers, both of them wonderful in their own ways. He's acutely aware that he doesn't—so far in his life—seem to be measuring up to either of his examples. His children regard him with ill-disguised contempt. He sees his son, Vernon, growing into a life of screwing up; Phil thinks he's at least partly responsible, and it's breaking his heart. When children screw up—thank God I don't have this problem!—there's always the question, Who do you blame, them or yourself? Phil blames himself. But he's only the dad. He doesn't exercise the real authority over what's going on with his kids. It's horrible for him.

L.S.: In this novel, I see elements of people we know or are related to. With *There Will Never Be Another You,* I'm thinking specifically of Harvard and Dash, to whom you dedicated the book. Generally speaking, how do you take the traits of real people and turn them into characters? More specifically, how are Dash and Harvard present in this novel?

C.S.: Harvard was an old boyfriend of mine, a second father to you—he adored you—and Dash is my younger daughter Clara's beautiful autistic son, who was about five when I began to write the book. Harvard's soul lives in Phil; Dash's spirit informs Vernon. Harvard was a bachelor, overweight, bumptious, jolly, and depressed—not physically like Dr. Philip Fuchs at all. Dash is affectionate, thin as a rail, otherworldly, not at all like the mean and angry Vernon. But Harvard didn't fit in his life; neither does Phil. And both Vern and Dash face a dubious, iffy future. More generally, when I "use" a person from real life in a fictional narrative, I take what I consider to be a person's "soul," body-snatch it, and put it into another person's body, or life. Sometimes, I must say, that method works better than other times.

L.S.: How much of you is in Edith?

C.S.: There's a certain first-person narrator who wanders through some of my novels, *The Rest Is Done with Mirrors, Mothers, Daughters, Golden Days,* and now *Another You,* who certainly resembles me. That voice changes as I change. But Edith isn't me. She weighs half as much as I do and she's ten years younger. She's more sophisticated. (But I'm more educated.) In my mind, she owes something, maybe, to both your grandmas. She's been a traditional wife, and now she doesn't have a husband. She's crabbier than I am, I think. She's come to a point in life where she just throws up her hands in dismay.

L.S.: Your last two novels—*There Will Never Be Another You* and *The Handyman*—have men as main characters. What are the challenges of getting into a man's mind?

C.S.: I think the main challenge was to try as hard as I could to let go of my preconceptions about men in general. In my life, they've often been "cute," or "tyrants," or "saints," whatever. But in both *The Handyman* and *Another You,* I just took the position that they were *actual human beings,* as human as I am. Then, when I did that, I had to "notice," as we used to say, that men have a terribly hard time just making a go of it in this society. They have to be strong, they should try to excel in what it is they do for a living, they have to deal with the myriad needs and whining of women in their lives, and they've got the incessant distractions of their dicks, which often have their own agendas. They're often as dazed and confused as we are, but they can't admit it. So I went with that. And no guy has complained!

L.S.: Vernon is an unexpectedly pivotal character. Was that planned, or did it evolve?

C.S.: You don't see too many children in novels—unless they're in children's books or written from a child's point of view. I think there's a fear of getting the dialogue wrong or just generally hitting a wrong note. I loved playing with Eloise and Vern. Eloise is just awful, and she likes it that way. She thinks she's been born into the wrong family, and she's right. Vern is something else. He's the wild card—the unsolvable problem, the thing none of us can figure out. He's literally a lost soul. I guess—in my novels, if not in my life—I like to give those people an unexpected, entirely unexpected, happy ending.

L.S.: I love the dead cats on the UCLA campus. They're so creepy and scary. Where on earth did you get that idea? Do you have something against cats?

C.S.: Oh, Lisa, you know I *love* cats!

L.S.: I know. Clara put me up to it! She says lots of people have asked you this.

C.S.: That's true. There's something creepy about an animal in the wrong place. Remember when we all lived in Topanga Canyon and went on a rampage against gophers and nearly killed ourselves in the process? Or how your own life has been plagued by tree rats? I'll never forget a classified monograph I read from the Rand Corporation that said the life of Los Angeles depended on whether or not the plague-infested squirrels in the Santa Monica Mountains ever came down into town and said hi to our city squirrels, because then the whole metropolis would come down with bubonic plague. When animals around us start dying, that's the gypsy's warning. And we know there are *way* too many feral cats on the campus of UCLA!

L.S.: I've known you since you were twenty-one years old and watched you become a writer. Let's talk about writing and your body of work. Your love of jazz is well known, and it's often said that your writing is like a jazz riff. How does music—and jazz in particular—feature in your writing?

C.S.: One of the things I admire most about your writing is your ability to plot. I just don't have that! But when I think about it, you're right, I write a novel as a jazz piece. I do the first and last chapters first—the way a combo will play a tune, then each musician will improvise a solo on top of the chord changes of that tune, then they all come together again at the end, reprising the tune, but if it's been good, you'll "know" so much more about what the tune means at the end, be transformed by it. I just found out that Lester Young would turn his back to the audience and mumble the lyrics of a song to his musicians right before they played it, so they'd "know" what they were playing. The last section of *Another You* is meant to be like the reprise of the jazz standard that the novel is named after, on an album where Warne Marsh and Lee Konitz come together so beautifully for the last chorus. It's one of the prettiest, spookiest pieces of music I know.

L.S.: It seems to me that fear has often served as inspiration for your novels. In *Golden Days,* you dealt with the fear of nuclear annihilation. In *Making History*, you looked at what happens to a family when a child dies. And now, in *There Will Never Be Another You*, you've created a post-9/11 world where plagues and wars and other scary things are happening. Could you talk about the juxtaposition of worldwide terror with the terrors we experience in our daily lives? Is it easier to focus on the big terrors or the other way around?

C.S.: Oh, Lisa, you know I'm terrified of everything! I took a test in high school about being fearful and scored ten out of ten. I devoted a whole chapter in *Golden Days* to "How Scared We Were." I'm scared of abandonment, the Bomb, riding in cars, being the last one chosen on the team, and scared when you kids would get sick. Just looking at our president's face on television scares me, before he even opens his mouth. I know it's never going to be good news. Then, being scared makes me mad. I get so *furious* with government, or bullies, or threats. And I think there's no real line of demarcation between the "Big" or "Little" things that threaten us. During the anthrax scare, I'd just look at the envelopes on the table, knowing I'd have to open them but not liking the prospect at all. The thing is, I'd bet a million other people are as scared as I am. I do know that fear—and finally getting over some of it—is what powers my books.

L.S.: You were born in Los Angeles and have lived here your entire life. All of your novels take place in Los Angeles. What is it about this city that keeps you writing about it?

C.S.: As you know, I have an elderly boyfriend who taunts me about being a "regional" writer. He just doesn't get it—that I *want* to be a regional writer! When I did my doctoral dissertation on the Hollywood novel, there were literally hundreds of them, written by hundreds of people, but only three guys at that time, forty years ago, had written about Los Angeles. When I was young and dopey, I'd fret about how life had already passed me by—I'd never get to be in Paris in the twenties, where people were doing wonderful work and having so much fun. I'd missed it. Then I thought, What if I get to be in Los Angeles in the twenties of the twenty-first century? And later, people will gnash their teeth because they weren't here, creating and having fun. I love this place more than I can say. It's huge and inexplicable and mysterious. I wish I had another lifetime to explore it.

L.S.: *Making a Literary Life* is the best book I've read on writing and how to become a writer. And I'm not just saying that because you're my mom! I know the answers to this, but could you tell the readers about a typical writing day for you? Do you have any rituals that you follow or particular music you listen to?

C.S.: A typical writing day. When it's going well, after breakfast I go out on the balcony where I live, or sit on the couch or at the kitchen table, pick up a felt-tip pen and a pad of white paper and write a thousand words—or revise for about two hours. I usually put on Van Morrison, turned down very low. I like the chanting, repetitive pieces he does, like when he'll sing, "my waitress, my waitress, my waitress," about fifteen times over, and I like his magical quality. I can stand any distraction, I can write anywhere. I love when people call up, because then I get a break. I don't like to work more than two hours. But I have to say, there are other days when I'll hang out and mope, or read, or procrastinate and get anxious—do anything to keep from writing.

L.S.: You've given me tons of advice about how to start and keep writing even in the face of disappointments and skepticism from others. When you started writing, there were very few writers in Los Angeles, let alone women writers. Because of that, it seems to me that you faced a lot of obstacles. How have you managed to stay true to your artistic vision?

C.S.: You just do it, that's all. Every writer has to be a little bit delusional about his or her work. We have to know it's good. Even if we hate it, we have to know it's good. Perseverance, stubbornness, has everything to do with keeping on. When I started writing, I was the wrong age, too young, the wrong gender—not all that many women were writing for a living then—and on the wrong coast, the west one. But you just have to put all that aside and go on working. I remember when you were working on your family history, *On Gold Mountain,* a lot of elders on the Chinese side of your family didn't want you to do it. They grumbled and even threatened. But you just went ahead and did it, and now they're so proud. Stubbornness doesn't guarantee success—we both know that. But at the very least, it gives you the experience of writing, which is the most important thing.

L.S.: You've always written about families, and you've borrowed a lot from our family. Over the years, I've certainly recognized your parents, my dad and my stepfather, and my sister and me in various characters. In your early work, you could sometimes be cruel and unforgiving, especially to the mothers. In your more recent novels, you've been more kind, empathetic, and benevolent to your characters, even though they're just as wacky and clueless. Could you talk a bit about that evolution for you as a writer and as a person? Similarly, in your early novels, you could be—and forgive me for saying this—a bit harsh and bitter. These days, critics and readers call you warm, witty, and wise, which you are! How have you been able to find humor in the most difficult circumstances?

C.S.: It's no secret that I had a pretty gothic childhood. It's a tire-some fact that my mother hated my sister and me, really couldn't bear the sight of us, and kicked us both out of her house when we were just sixteen. It's hard to be attacked for simply existing when you're a child. My sister turned to drugs very early on and died young. But remember when I was talking about fear turning into anger? By the time I was sixteen I was so angry that I didn't even know I was angry. It was my key to survival. I knew the world was a terrible place. I lived alone in furnished rooms, worked for a Ph.D., was *convinced* that I wouldn't end up like my mother, who I perceived of as both a monster and a victim. The irony was: I was already like my mother. I was married twice, when I was still young, to your father and to Clara's dad. I feel sorry for those guys. I was enraged all the time. We had a lot of fun, but my fury was just under the surface. When I first started writing—say, for *TV Guide*—if they wanted a hatchet job, they'd ask me, because I could only see flaws and wickedness. You and Clara suffered for this, and I apologize to you both from the bottom of my heart.

Then—and I think of it as a lifelong journey—I began to get a grip. I found a wonderful therapist. We stumbled into—how em-barrassing now!—prosperity seminars, which didn't make us rich but let us all have a huge amount of fun. Harvard was very kind to us. Then the wife of the director of my doctoral dissertation died. He waited a year, then came to call, and we were together for twenty-seven years. John Espey, a terrific writer and a won-derful man, taught me that life, for all its cruelty, was mar-velously interesting and beautiful. I started writing at the end of my second marriage, when I was absolutely frantic with rage and fear. But the writing saved me, you girls saved me, therapy, semi-nars, and Mr. Espey saved me. So, over the course of thirty-five years, my characters changed from wacky and monstrous to wacky and clueless, limited in many ways, as we all are. But capable of redemption, as we all are. Does that sound pious enough?

L.S.: People who are reading this might be curious about our relationship. You're a writer and I'm a writer. But what people may not know is that your dad was a writer and my sister, Clara, is also a writer. So here we are with three generations of writers. Can you talk a little about Grandpa George? In what ways did he shape you—for good and for bad—as a writer?

C.S.: Ah, Grandpa George. My dad. He left when I was eleven, damaging my mother for life. But he himself had had a monstrous childhood. When he was fourteen his mother killed herself—blew her head off with a shotgun—and he was the one to discover the body. The family story is that she'd left a note accusing her husband of hideous sexual excess. Daddy grew up to be a Clintonian ladies' man, collecting many wives and girl-friends. But along with that, he loved literature, wanted more than anything to be a writer. He was too shy, though. Perhaps he couldn't take the rejection. He was insanely funny; it was his way of coping with pain. He wrote columns for neighborhood newspapers, dreamed about writing the great American novel. Then, when I was thirty-five and working as an expert witness in pornography trials, his fourth wife had a son. I went down to help with the baby. I was in the kitchen with a stack of porn, he picked up a book, idly leafed through it, and said, "I can do better than this." It was the beginning of his literary career. He was sixty-nine and went on to publish seventy-three volumes of hardcore pornography. I've only read four, but I know they were spoofs of different genres and howlingly funny. I understand them now to be the end of a lifelong argument he was having with his dead mom—that there's nothing wrong with sex, that it's part of the human condition, and we should all try and lighten up about it. I learned from him how to love words for their own sake, to mask rage with humor, and to try to be a good person, even if it doesn't always work out as planned.

L.S.: We talk on the phone every day about our work, and we do a lot of speaking events together. Can you talk about how we support each other yet keep our identities and careers separate?

C.S.: I think the work has been a wonderful blessing for both of us—and for Clara too, though she's become more of an autism advocate. It's given us something to talk about and strive for outside of ourselves. I don't see us as ever having been in competition. For one thing, we're doing entirely different things. You write about China, for instance, I write about L.A. And our voices are entirely different. It's like the difference between eggs Benedict and lemon meringue pie: they both use eggs, they're both yellow and white, but you would never mistake one for the other. I'm more proud of your success than I could ever say. Aside from our separate creative work, there's the other stuff we can do together—go to each other's signings and talk to people in line, address the announcements and invitations when either one of us has a book coming out. I love those times we get to spend together. We don't fight, because we're busy working! It's really, really nice.

L.S.: Readers of this wouldn't forgive me if I didn't ask what you're working on now. What's next?

C.S.: You gave me the idea, you rascal! I keep talking, these days, about my women's group, which has been together for thirteen years, longer than some marriages. We were rowdies in our youth; now we're sedate old ladies, but not really. You suggested I write about not *them,* but about women like us, who mostly have lost our husbands, or struggle with illness, or deal with "wacky and clueless" grown children, and still manage to have more than their share of adventures. These women have careers, come from all over the world. They have lovely lives. At the same time, death is the uninvited guest at each of their elegant lunches. This will be a romantic celebration of female friendship that—in my more grandiose moments—I think could echo the history of women in America for the last fifty years. The title: *Love, Death, Lunch*.

QUESTIONS AND
TOPICS FOR DISCUSSION

1. Early in the novel, Edith says, "Then the curtain went up for me . . . and I saw the world. . . . I learned about the world, what it was made of. I can't say I liked it, or that any of it has done me any good. All I can do now is divide the world between those who know and those who don't" (page 14). Who else in *There Will Never Be Another You* has had the curtain go up? What caused it to rise?

2. On page 16, Edith claims that she is stuck. What does she mean? Is she still stuck at the end of the novel?

3. When Phil attends the first meeting of the secret medical team, Colonel Davies waves away Phil's concerns about his lack of qualifications and says, "We've been looking into you. You're our man." Why do you think Phil is selected for the job?

4. On page 41, Edith says, "He *must* know—he's selling himself short—that he could be so much more than he is." Why has Phil settled, in his career, his marriage, and his happiness? What made him aim so low?

5. Did something go wrong with Vernon and Eloise, or does their behavior fall within the spectrum of that of "normal" children? Is anyone (or anything) to blame for Vernon's poor grades and misbehavior, or for Eloise's disdain for her family?

6. When Phil and Felicia argue about having another baby, Phil wants to say, "Don't you think this world-situation thing is a little out of *control*? . . . Do you think we both don't know Eloise is sneaking out at night? Don't you know I fool around sometimes? Don't we both know that something's up with Vernon, something's *really* up? So isn't the whole thing a fiasco by now?" (page 66). So much of Phil and Felicia's life together seems to have happened *to* them, as though they have had no impact on the trajectory of their experiences. How did Phil lose control so completely? Why does he feel so powerless to make things better? Has a collective sense of helplessness contributed to the state of our world?

7. Following one of their mandatory training sessions, Phil asks his friend Jack, "What I want to know . . . is how did we get into this? What is it that we did? As a country, I mean?" (page 109). What do you think America has done to contribute to, or cause, the current political climate? After Phil poses this grave question, he notes that, "There was the lobster in front of him, and lights flashing out to sea. Let it alone. Eat it." Why does See juxtapose the enjoyment of first-world comforts with fear and unease?

8. At the Palomino, Phil and Jack see a drunk man confront the government official who created a security plan that compromises citizens' rights. The Secret Service guard present says, "We have to pull together as a country. We have to put the good of the country over personal matters. Patriotism trumps the personal" (page 116). Do you agree with the guard? Or should we protect ourselves and our loved ones before we act on behalf of our country? Have the actions taken by our government made you feel more or less secure?

9. He barely whispered, close to her ear, " 'I wonder by my troth . . .' "

And she answered, in another world, " 'What thou and I didst . . .' "

And heard him, wondering, " 'Till we loved' " (page 129).

What brings Andrea and Danny together so immediately and intensely? What is the effect of this subplot woven through the book?

10. During the sounding of the alarm that goes off at the hospital, "it seemed to [Andrea] that something really big had happened, not just to her or to her mother and father. The past had been cut off somehow and they were already living in the future, all of them" (page 209). What has cut off the past and propelled everyone out of the present and into the future?

11. When Phil joins the *Andorra,* bringing Vern along with him, he is rescuing both his son and himself. When does Phil begin to consider getting out, and why does it seem to be the only option? Is Phil acting out of bravery or cowardice? Is he a hero, or is he just running away?

12. When *There Will Never Be Another You* was first published in hardcover, the spring of 2007 had not yet happened. It was set in the immediate future and "infused with the anxieties of the present" (*Publishers Weekly*). Does this sense of unease still ring true now? How long might *There Will Never Be Another You* seem like a novel set in the imminent future?

CAROLYN SEE, the author of ten books, has won both a Guggenheim and a Getty Fellowship and has served on the boards of the Modern Library, the National Book Critics Circle, and PEN Center USA West. She is Friday-morning book reviewer for *The Washington Post*. She lives in Pacific Palisades, California. She can be reached at csee@ucla.edu, and you can visit her website: www.carolynsee.com.